# FAMOUS IN MURRAYVILLE

## MARY VINE

Windtree
Press

FAMOUS IN MURRAYVILLE

Author Mary Vine

Published by Windtree Press in cooperation with Melland Publishing, LLC.

Windtree Press

Portland, Oregon

https://windtreepress.com

Melland Publishing, LLC

Caldwell, ID

http://mellandpublishing.com

Published in the United States of America

Publishing History

1st Edition 2020, Windtree Press

Print ISBN 978-1-952447-15-0

Ebook ISBN 978-1-952447-14-3

# CHAPTER 1

*F*aith Chadwick steered her car toward dark clouds looming in the distance. She watched the wind blow along the creek moving the ripples of water with a burst of power, and rip through a canopy of trees above the road.

Instead of five o'clock it looked more like the evening when the summer sun went down and blanketed the land with darkness. She couldn't get home fast enough.

Thunder pealed as she prepared to leave her car and enter the house. Even though she ran from the car, rain blew into her face, hair and suit. Once inside, she tried to shake the water off before letting out a breath of relief.

She was glad her dog Roger was in the sanctuary of his dog crate, so he wasn't wandering around the house frightened from the noise of the thunder.

Before she opened the crate, she hung her suit jacket on the coat rack behind the door. A loud thump from the direction of the kitchen, plus a growl from Roger, startled her.

Her father resided here, too, but he was gone for the

summer. Perhaps he'd made it home earlier than planned. No, he wouldn't be here without his car.

She started toward the kitchen catching her reflection in the hallway mirror as lightning flashed. Her normally golden hair looked white in the light that eerily made her face appear ashen, aging her beyond her twenty-five years.

"Dad? Dad, is that you?"

Her heart jumped when she heard the sound again and froze when she saw the back door moving back and forth in the wind. Yet, it was automatic for her to lock it, being a single woman, often alone. Her father wouldn't leave the back door open in this weather, either.

"Hello! Hello!" Her voice rang off the walls, sounding high and off pitch. She did a quick visual check of each room and then made it to the back door. Even above the sound of the rain, the crunch of rocky soil and snapping limbs told her something, no someone, walked nearby. She shut and locked the door and backed away.

Roger barked again, making her feel confident. Stealthily, she moved to the side of a window and peeked out the edge of the curtain. Not far from the house a man, clothed in a rain slicker, walked down the edge of her property and then onto the land adjacent to hers. The neighboring property belonged to the Bureau of Land Management and he had a right to be there, but this situation was a little too close for comfort. She didn't see a car or truck nearby and he couldn't have just appeared, but what really troubled her was he could've been in her home.

After grabbing a kitchen chair, she placed it near the window, but sat out of sight so she could spy on him. He stopped and looked back as if he knew she was there.

With fears renewed, Faith considered whether to call the sheriff, yet after a few minutes her heart calmed down and she felt safe in her home. The man was probably a hiker who lost his way. She, most likely, left the backdoor ajar and the powerful wind blew it open. It was summer after all, and last night she did have the door open to enjoy a cool breeze.

While chirping words of love to Roger, Faith grabbed a towel and wiped up the rainwater next to the door, then kicked off her shoes. She slipped her cell phone into her pocket, then searched the area from a few windows for signs of the hiker. He was nowhere to be found. The storm passed through as well.

Upon release, Roger went bounding out the front door, but squatted only briefly. Either the man had gone, or the possibility of thunder made Roger come right back in. Faith poured a touch of chicken broth in with dry dog food and set the dog bowl on the kitchen floor.

In her bedroom, Faith studied a few knickknacks askew on the nightstand, and the way one of her dresser drawers was not quite shut. She sat down on the bed and twisted her fingers until she'd convinced herself that she'd made a mountain out of a mole hill.

Roger came in the room licking his chops.

"I'm a little paranoid aren't I, Roger?"

His only answer was to sniff around the room, and she wondered if she was not so paranoid after all.

BRIEN MCGREW COULDN'T BELIEVE his good fortune. The very piece of ground he came to Northeast Oregon to find was available for a mining claim. That meant he didn't have to sneak around the property until he found what he came for. Everything was nice and legal. Yet, he didn't like the house that had sprung up over the years since he was twelve years old. He needed privacy for what he intended to do and the woman spying through the window troubled him. The thunder and pouring rain matched his mood.

The next day, Brien was back at his mining claim testing out his new shovel and realized that his recent college years at the gym helped with the work of digging. He'd stopped to wipe the sweat from his forehead, happy he'd just gotten a haircut, then noticed a dog running his way. The dog's long and lanky body moved quickly across the ground and he braced himself.

The dog, a male, sniffed around his legs then stepped back. His bark was not exactly threatening or welcoming. Abruptly, he stopped barking as if waiting for an answer from him.

"Good boy."

He barked again.

"Top of the morning to you."

He barked in reply and then moved closer to sniff. It was like the dog tried to have a conversation with him. A hello if he'd ever seen one and he couldn't help but smile.

His coat had the coloring of a German Shepherd, but his inward curling tail and face markings spoke of Malamute or some sort of sled dog. He didn't have the black snout of a German shepherd. Yet, somehow, he didn't get pert ears from either side of the family. His jug ears gave him character, Brien decided.

When the woman had come out of the house, the first thing Brien had noticed was her blonde hair catching the sun. Her white blouse was tucked into a fitted beige skirt.

She was a vision of beauty until she came near enough for him to notice the hiking boots and walking stick that spoiled her put together appearance. As a matter of fact, it was rather humorous to see her in boots, marching her way through the thicket.

Pretty or not, Brien didn't want company at his claim this

summer. To keep his perspective, he focused on the hiking boots as she moved closer.

"Hello there," she said, upon nearing.

"Hello, Ma'am."

"Roger minds well, usually. Sorry he's bothering you."

"He's fine. We were just having a little conversation here."

She raised her hand and Roger lay down next to her. "You aren't from around here, are you?"

The man squinted as if the sun was in his eyes, but she figured it had more to do with her question. It had taken her ten minutes of pacing to get the nerve to come over here after what she went through last night. So right now, she didn't particularly care if he was uncomfortable with her query.

Roger's departure from the house gave her a reason to stop by and the walking stick gave her added courage thinking she could hit him in a certain spot if she had to.

"No," he said.

Her thumb pointed over her shoulder. "Roger and I live right next door."

"Yes, I see that."

He stuck out a hand, very business-like. "My name is Brien McGrew."

She shook his hand firmly. "My name's Faith."

He briefly turned and looked at something behind him but didn't say anything more.

She, too, scanned the area behind him, but came up lacking. "How did you get here? I didn't see a car or truck."

"My four-wheeler is in the back," he said, pointing to the woods.

After she nodded, he said, "I have a claim here, ma'am."

She gripped her walking stick. "Right here where you're standing?"

"Yes."

She couldn't have him so close to her home. She liked living in a house made and placed with privacy in mind. Faith didn't like to be found after hours by someone wanting to tell her how to run the town. As the town mayor, that was her job.

Besides, he was too good looking, and she didn't see a ring. The next thing she knew, she'd be buying binoculars and offering him lemonade. No, he would disrupt her quiet life too much.

"Will you be here often?" She crossed an arm over her chest and waited.

He crossed both of his arms. "Why do you ask?"

That was probably better than saying none of your business, she decided. "Uh … it floods in the spring."

He lifted an eyebrow. "Really? I don't see signs of it."

"We had a wet spring this year, just about everywhere in the state did, seems like."

"Anything else I need to know?"

"Yes. Snow drifts in the winter. I can hardly make it home some days." Well, that was the truth.

"That doesn't bother me. Especially since I'll probably not be here past the summer." After a moment of silence, he added, "What's the town of Murrayville like?"

Maybe it wasn't all year, and she should be thankful, but she didn't want him to spoil her summer either. "Oh, the mayor is screwed up and has been causing lots of problems in town. You may not even be able to get the kind of permits you need. And the people aren't very friendly," she said with a big smile and hugged the stick to her side.

"Well, I have the permit I need, and I want to keep to myself anyway."

That's all Faith could think to say and since he apparently didn't want to say anything else, she turned to go while wondering if she had the power to take back a mining permit. Probably not. She patted the side of her thigh and Roger followed her home.

ONE AT A TIME, Marty Walker took his late wife's clothes out of their shared closet and divided them up by garment. He had no tender feelings about any of the pieces but only thought of the process as a job he needed to do before getting ready to sell the house.

As he worked, he thought about why they moved to Murrayville in the first place. He'd spent some time in the nearby forest searching for gold. By the time he had accumulated enough dirt to pan he found gold flakes and a nugget, and sequentially, his wife Nancy was offered a good paying job in Murrayville. He'd made enough for him to take a part-time job at the library and resume searching for gold.

Now finally, she was gone. Certainly, Nancy had value to him when she was alive. She brought home an adequate paycheck and was a good wife until she was diagnosed with stage four cancer. He'd give her credit for working as long as she could, but then she got to a place where she had to remain home. A good thing that happened was the library promoted him to the very top of the library's employment ladder, in hopes of giving him more money to take care of his wife.

Finally, Marty had used up all of Nancy's money for her care along with his gold, but he had nothing left to give her now, so he placed a pillow over her face one morning and shortened her suffering, and his as well.

Marty had already found his next wife, but she didn't know it yet. He watched her walk along Main Street in Murrayville and then from afar whenever he could. Nancy had what you would call a cute face, but this woman was beautiful in every way, and he started to prepare for the day that he identified himself to her as his soulmate.

~

SATURDAY MORNING, Faith looked out her bedroom window at the junipers, pines and rocky crags she loved. *Why wouldn't someone else want to be out here enjoying themselves?* she asked herself. Faith could only hope though that Brien didn't mine right up to her property line. He couldn't very well set up a high banker on his claim as the creek wasn't close enough, she realized.

The day brought thunder and the new neighbor. This time he came in a white Dodge pickup followed by a gravel truck and another truck pulling a cat behind it. The three men huddled together, Brien pointed and nodded, and the cat-man prepared to unload the cat.

Faith sighed, seeing the path he'd chosen was too close for her comfort. She couldn't watch anymore and went to the kitchen for breakfast.

Her plan for the day had included organizing her closets, but all she wanted to do now was linger over her pancakes and bacon. At length, she thought of the stack of to-be-read books she had and planned to read one.

Faith cleaned up and pulled her hair back into a ponytail, then settled in her favorite chair to read. As usual, Roger settled on top of her feet.

*The man came out of nowhere,* she read. *He just appeared at the edge of the forest. His dark hair hit the collar of his jean jacket and his jeans set low on his hips.*

"Oh, for Pete's sake," she said and shut the book.

Roger let out a hello bark after approaching the window. She joined him at the window, and she saw Brien, alone now. He had on a jean jacket and of course his jeans fit low at his waist. "Oh, for Pete's sake," she said again, only wanting to be alone, truly alone, but even her book betrayed her.

She'd just go out there and see what he was up to and then he'd start talking and he'd be boring, or sound like an idiot, and she'd feel better. He'd not gain her attention or thoughts, in no time she'd be back organizing the closets, and all would be right with her world.

Brien had sensed her presence at the window before he saw her, and now he sensed her again, a moment before he could hear her footsteps.

Today Faith dressed casually, far different than he'd seen her last. Upon nearing, he could see a face bare of make-up. He liked watching her thick ponytail swing back and forth and the natural beauty of her.

He looked for a ring and didn't see one, and then he momentarily closed his eyes to keep his thoughts from going where he didn't think they should go. The last thing he wanted was interference. No one could know what he was doing here, no matter how pretty.

The sun broke through the clouds, shimmered through the trees, and highlighted Brien's hair giving him an almost angelic glow.

"Oh, for Pete's sake," Faith muttered.

"I'm sorry, I didn't hear you," he said, as she neared.

"Good morning," she said instead.

"Good morning."

Roger sniffed Brien's knees and then barked a hello. Brien patted his head.

"Looks like you're going to mine here after all." It was a stupid remark, she knew, but the words just came out.

"No one else mentioned any flooding, so I went ahead with it," he said with a half-smile.

"Hmmm. What's going on here?" she asked with a sweep of her hand.

9

"I need a level section to put a trailer. Perfectly level now."

"A trailer?"

"Yes, a travel trailer. I presented my plans here to the BLM and they approved it."

She wanted to say something negative, but instead said, "Thanks for your efficiency." After a few minutes of staring at her shoes, she said, "Will it be large enough for your family?"

"Are you trying to figure out if I'm married or are you just nosy?"

She searched his face but didn't see any malice there. She put a hand to her chest. "I want to know who is living next to me, is all," she answered, probably a little too dramatically.

He smiled. "That's fair, I suppose. It's only going to be me here this summer, maybe fall."

The streak of sun in his eyes made his brown eyes almost an amber color. Faith still didn't want a neighbor so close, no matter how easy on her eyes. She wanted no one to know what she did with her private time, wasn't that the reason she moved out of town? The last thing she needed was wagging tongues completely marring her reputation in this town.

Yet, his words didn't give her any encouragement. If he didn't want to release any real information about himself, then he'd hardly want to learn more about her. It hurt her ego momentarily, but it soon subsided as she remembered what she really wanted from this neighbor. Nothing.

Now, what was he saying? He said that he would be living here alone.

"If you'll be needing anything-" She couldn't believe the words slipped out of her mouth. She need not encourage him.

"I won't need a thing," he quickly added.

"Okay," she finally said. *Good.*

With a smile of satisfaction and a swish of her ponytail,

she'd turned and started back to the house, hopefully to clean out her closet this time. Thankfully, Roger came with her.

EVEN WITH FAITH'S head stuck in the closet she heard the noise.

Roger pushed into the closet. "That isn't thunder," she said to him. "No … blasting. Brien's blasting!"

# CHAPTER 2

Faith ran to the window but could only see Brien's truck. After a minute of deliberation, she decided she'd have to get closer to see what he'd done.

Roger would be safer at home, she believed, so she grabbed some dog treats, threw them in his kennel and closed the door behind him. "Good boy. I'll be right back. I hope."

Her concern turned to anger as she marched through the thicket. No, she didn't suffer fools kindly. He needed a permit for blasting, for goodness sake. She certainly didn't need a hole in her house, or worse.

Brien held a shovel, moving dirt and rocks away from the blasting site. He heard her coming and inclined his head toward her.

"What are you doing?"

"Hold on, neighbor," he said with a frown. "Things are okay over here."

"You're blasting."

"Good assumption."

"Really?" After a moment, she added, "You need some sort of permit for this, don't you? What if you hit my house?"

His eyes narrowed. "I wasn't aiming at your house."

She put her hands on her hips.

He leaned on the shovel. "I have the paperwork to do this. It's in the glove box of the truck if you want to look at it."

"What are you doing, anyway?" she asked, palms up.

"I'm mining."

"I think you'll find more of what you're looking for around Murray Creek."

"No, I don't think so."

She followed his eyes. "What's that smiley face thingy etched in the rock there?"

He did look at her now, concern evident in his wide eyes.

When he didn't say anything, she said, "There's markings on the rock. Looks like an alien's been here."

"A vivid imagination you have there. No, more like some kids carved something."

He moved closer to her, shoulders back, blocking her view.

"Are you finished with the blasting?" she asked.

"Hard to say. I may have to do some more. I'll be careful. I'll follow the rules."

"Humph."

She walked away; head held high. Faith thought she had the upper hand here, but she didn't. The claim was his for now, his dream come true, and he had about six months to find what he's looking for.

"Aliens," he said aloud and chuckled. She had no idea what was behind the old etching, so he was pretty sure she didn't pose a threat to him.

ROGER FOLLOWED A BUTTERFLY. His ears flopped as he happily hopped around weeds and bushes in the distance. Faith sat on her porch swing, enjoying the sunny day to the very end. She slowly sipped a glass of lemonade and considered how heavenly it was to sit quietly after listening to council members thrash out ways to promote new business in Murrayville. Even though the town needed to bring in visitors and money to area businesses, their petty arguments about how to make it happen made her stare longingly at the exit sign.

Yet, she knew she could work under pressure. She focused on the notes she'd taken for herself, highlighting the important points, and then set about putting together two committees to work up ideas. They would talk to professionals, take data and then present their findings during the next meeting. But she would go with each group, not that she didn't trust them, but she took the job seriously and wanted to be sure that everything was copacetic during her time as mayor.

Momentarily, she pressed the rim of the cool glass against her upper lip and smiled, then frowned. She hadn't realized the correlation until now, but as a middle school teacher, she'd put her students in small groups and given them homework. Most of the people in the council meetings didn't mingle together outside of the meetings but she hoped they could learn from each other just as her reluctant students had.

Faith downed the rest of her lemonade, called to Roger, and changed into shorts and a t-shirt. Under the bedroom window, she dropped dirty clothes into a hamper. Looking up, she saw a crack in the lower portion of the window and a few pebbles along the narrow trim.

"No! He blasted again."

She slipped on her tennis shoes and headed out of the

house with determined footfalls. She walked along the side to check for further damage but only spotted a few broken limbs on the roof of her house.

Brien wasn't there, but that didn't stop her from looking at the hole he was set on making.

It looked to her like Brien tried to break up a large rock. He'd managed to crack it pretty good, enough to send parts of it flying.

Why didn't she see any signs of gold mining? No dredges of any kind, not even a gold pan anywhere in sight. Did he take the earth he'd plowed through to another site to dredge? It was possible, she supposed.

She stepped closer to the rock that had the crude drawing of a face carved in it. Now, more shapes were revealed. What in the world did someone use to make the drawings? she wondered.

With her index finger, she traced the markings. She didn't know what was communicated here, but she highly doubted a teenager did this as she didn't find the f-word anywhere.

A pictograph maybe? Perhaps the circle was not a face after all but the sun, and could the dots below be pointing to something?

Faith still thought it looked more alien than human, yet she wondered what Brien thought of this. He certainly had an opinion, as he blasted right in front of it.

She didn't have to wonder long, because he drove onto the gravel of his newly formed driveway.

"What's going on?" he asked in a perturbed tone.

"Well, that's what I want to know. It appears your blasting reached my bedroom window and left a nice crack in it."

He shook his head. "That shouldn't have happened."

"That's exactly what I thought," she shot back, hands on hips.

"No, I mean the way I set it up, it shouldn't have hit your window."

"Well, come look."

She led the way and didn't look back at him, hoping all the while that he'd take responsibility for the damage, and not continue to deny it.

This woman was swiftly becoming a thorn in his flesh by snooping around his claim and then declaring he'd cracked her window. Who did she think she was, the town boss?

He stomped his shoes on her doormat and followed her into the house. She made a beeline to her bedroom, apparently not concerned about him coming in at all. If she'd been thinking, she'd have taken him to the outside to look in.

His eyes scanned the king-size bed first. It looked quite cozy with a white comforter and colorful pillows, including two shiny ones in the shape of a heart.

He believed that either meant an invitation for intimacy or a warning that the women wanted commitment. Humph, like it mattered to him. He made every effort to move his head toward the window and focus on Faith.

Her face reddened, so she probably caught him staring at the bed. She should have thought about that before she brought him in here.

"I see the crack, but how do I know you didn't do it?"

"Can you tell me how I would have done this, huh?"

"Pressed against it too hard when you were staring out?"

If possible, her face turned redder. After a moment she said, "I have a new neighbor, of course I'm curious."

He looked up from the window. "Curious?"

"Yes. Aren't you curious about your new neighbor?"

"Not really, no. I plan to keep to myself."

"You'll be the perfect neighbor then."

Brien hadn't realized that they both had their arms crossed until he'd moved his to his pockets.

Faith took a deep breath. "The reason I was at your property is because I thought you were blasting again, and sure enough you were."

"Yes, I did blast again. So?"

"So, look out the window and you will see broken rock, and limbs below."

"I can't really see what you're talking about from this side of the window. Why didn't you just show me from the outside?"

"Uh … "

"Was there a reason you wanted me in your bedroom?" he asked, basically to knock her off her high horse. Brien turned to look at the bed.

*Well, of all the nerve*, she thought.

"Humph." She pointed her finger at him. "I happened to think that you could see the damage better from this angle. From this side of the window."

"I can't really see what caused it from here as I tried to state before," he said, voice rising.

How could someone be so handsome and be so rude?

"Come on." She headed for the front porch. He followed quietly at her heels to the other side of the bedroom window.

She pointed up to the window hoping he realized what she'd said was true, that you can't see as close to the window as you could from the inside.

But he was already looking at broken branches and pieces of rock that she knew looked perfectly out of order in her manicured yard.

"Well?"

He picked up a branch and studied the broken end, then he sighed, good and hard. "I'll have the window fixed. The next time will be better."

"Thank you. The next time?"

"I have a claim here. I can dig down further if I want."

"For Pete's sake, why?"

"I thought I told you. Mining. I have a tape to measure your window in my toolbox. I'll be right back."

Back to Faith's bedroom, again. It wouldn't be so bad if she wasn't so good looking. He certainly didn't need a broken window, or a complication like her. Not to mention that he needed to be alone, he had the next six months planned out and spending extra money for damages was not part of it. Tomorrow he'd start digging with a shovel, make him think harder about making sure he didn't mess up again.

"Let me help," she said.

Faith was in the way, and Brien accidently brushed the side of her body when she came between his arm and the bedroom window. He couldn't move his arm back fast enough.

"Excuse me. I'm good here. I got it."

She still stood nearby hovering and staring.

"Can you get me a scrap of paper to write the measurements on?" He'd remember but writing it down would keep her busy.

"Oh. Sure."

When she left, he glanced around the room again. A piece of black material peaked out of a drawer. Black lace looked like. He groaned.

Faith liked watching him, the move of the muscles in his arms as he reached around the window to measure it.

He'd been in her bedroom two times now. She'd better not get used to seeing him here, she told herself.

She wanted this finished quickly, so she could go back to her solitary life. "Can you give me a timeline on the window?"

"Sooner the better," he said as if reading her thoughts.

"That's my take on it, too," she replied and walked toward the door as a signal it was time to leave.

When he did leave, her thoughts had him right back in the house. He was just so darn cute. She shook her head. Yet, not cute enough to divert her away from the fact that he was blasting and damaging her house. And, he didn't show one lick of interest in her.

∿

"MISS FAITH. How are you doing this week?" asked Rose Langley.

Faith looked up from a file on her desk to see the eighty-one-year-old standing across from her. Rose took a chair adjacent from Faith and ran a gnarled and knotted hand down the skirt of her dress.

"Good morning, Rose. I'm just fine, thank you."

It was a routine Faith expected, a standing appointment each Monday morning at nine o'clock sharp.

"Beautiful morning."

Faith nodded, straightened a small stack of manila files on her desk, then slid them aside to give the woman her full attention.

"Didn't see you in town over the weekend."

"No. I stayed home and took it easy," Faith said.

"Tsk. You won't get a man that way, you know."

"I suppose you could say I took a weekend off from the hunt."

Rose looked her in the eye. "I was over at the library Saturday. There's a guy works over there named Marty."

"Yes, I know who that it is. Seems like a nice guy."

"He is a nice guy. Widower you know."

"Oh," Faith said, her lips rounded.

"Well?"

"I think you should keep looking, Rose. With the number

19

of people in this town, I'm sure you can find someone more suitable to me."

Rose rubbed the back of her head as if she could push the falling hairs back into her short white ponytail. "Humph. You chose the last two times and where did that get you? It got you a couple of cowards. Couldn't even stand up to the town's foolishness."

She had a point, but Faith didn't want to discuss it with her. Again. Usually Rose asked if she could do something for her in the office, but not today.

"I have a few files here, if you'd like to work."

"Oh, not today. My ankles are bothering me, and I have to walk on over to Evelyn's and visit for a spell. She'll be making my lunch."

"Evelyn's making you lunch. That's nice. Sorry about your ankles."

"Evelyn doesn't cook anymore. Humph. She'll have bologna sandwiches and Fig Newtons. She's stuck in the 1960s is what she is. Back then that was a treat."

Faith smiled, trying not to laugh as Rose was serious.

"She'll be wanting to talk about you."

"Tell her work is going fine and I'm healthy."

"Didn't say happy, I noticed." Rose stood up. "I'll keep my eye out for you while I'm out and about."

Faith wondered what man she'd talk about next week. "Thanks for caring, Rose. Enjoy your visit with Evelyn."

FROM THE FRONT window of the town's bookstore, Marty watched the sway of Faith's hips as she took the sidewalk to her car.

He'd watched her many times since her last boyfriend left town. Her movements were predictable, from her trips to the bank and post office, to Friday nights at the Murrayville Roadhouse, her favorite hangout.

Up to now she'd never given him more than a quick smile, but that was going to change. He'd been patient and quiet for too long, and that kind of behavior didn't get him anywhere. He needed a new plan, one that would make her sit up and take notice of him once and for all.

On the way home from work, Faith thought about Rose and smiled, then she sobered thinking about her last boyfriend.

*"Do I have spinach in my teeth?" Mark asked Faith.*

*She looked up from her salad. "No."*

*"Well, I'm being watched, and I don't know why."*

*Between bites, Faith looked around the Murrayville Roadhouse. "They're just curious about us, is all."*

*"Do the people of Murrayville have nothing else to do?" he asked with a sigh.*

*"Famous in a Murrayville, I guess. Don't let it bother you. They'll look down at their food sooner or later." She laid her fork down. "Want to dance?"*

*"Sure."*

*Heads bobbing, shoulders swerving, idle chatter. Patron's cleared the way as if a prince and princess walked through.*

On the last part of her drive home, Faith refocused. She'd spent far too much time thinking about the past. Her life was just fine as it was. She had a job she'd wanted for a long time, a house in the country she loved, and big loveable Roger waiting for her at home. Besides, soon her father would be home and that gave her life balance as much as anything could. She was nothing but thankful for the life she had.

Shortly after she got home, Brien came to her door. He introduced an elderly man named Joe.

"You look familiar," said Joe, rubbing his chin with a hand."

"I've heard that before," she said with a smile. She truly had, a few thought she was a cashier at their favorite store or worked in their doctor's office. She thought it daunting more than humorous as the townspeople should remember their mayor.

The two of them set off to replace the window. She stayed clear by fixing a salad for dinner.

She wished, a little too late, that she'd had a chance to change out of her suit into something more comfortable. Her topknot gave her a headache, so she shook her hair loose. She sat down with the newspaper and salad and by the time she was finished, they were, too.

They stopped right in front of the high heels she'd kicked off. With a hand she reached down and scooted them out of the way. She looked up to catch Brien giving her the once over. He made eye contact, but it was Joe who spoke.

"The window's in, ma'am. Looks good and a duplicate of what you had. We'll be going now."

They shuffled out with tools and then the cracked window, which was now in two parts.

Brien leaned on his shovel and wiped his forehead with his shirtsleeve. The manual labor made him feel like he'd accomplished something today. Besides the reward of a job well done, he had a workout without paying a cent. Instead of a gym packed full of sweaty bodies in the big city, he smelled the pines and the fresh country air. He'd have to say he enjoyed coming to the country after all, instead of thinking he'd be joining primitive society.

He found the people of Murrayville to be a friendly

bunch. Many an old boy wanted to talk for hours about who found gold, when and where. He suspected many of the stories were true, yet embellished, reminding him of fish stories where the fish got bigger with each telling.

A few of the men reminded him of his grandfather, the reason he was here in the first place. Only his plan was for Pops to be right here digging beside him. Trouble was he'd gone to college so long that Pops didn't live long enough to see graduation, let alone work on this claim with him.

They'd talked of this time for years, how they'd work together and get rich. Pops said the gold they'd find would pay off his college debt and a good start in life. Brien tried to remember what Pops wanted for himself, but he came up blank.

From working alone for this short while, he realized that Pops was in it for the companionship. He missed him so much and wished he could share this very moment with the old man.

His luck had been holding out too, now he'd found more signs. As a matter of fact, the only problem he'd come up against was the neighbor lady.

Pops did leave him a little money. Good thing because, besides the trailer, he needed to buy one new window.

He wondered if any of the old boys in town knew much about Faith, a woman living to the right of nowhere, all alone. Brien felt uneasy around her, as she appeared to feel around him, and needed to find out more about her.

FAITH CAME home to a quiet evening. Whether Brien blasted or not, she didn't see any evident damage.

After a couple of tacos, she ran like a gerbil on her treadmill, showered and put on a terrycloth robe. Last, she picked up the book she'd started to read the other night.

A vehicle traveling nearby drew her from the page.

She got up in time to see Brien leaving. She hadn't seen him earlier, so he must have parked further away from the house.

She wondered where he went, if he had a place in town. Where was this trailer he planned to bring to the claim? She knew he didn't need a permit, so what was the holdup?

After throwing her terrycloth robe on the bed, she slipped into jeans and a t-shirt and grabbed a flashlight. It wasn't quite nine o'clock, and there was a bit of daylight left but probably not enough to see down into the hole.

It was a pleasant night, the air cooling as the sun set. In the distance, she could hear a dog bark. Roger lifted his head to listen but didn't respond in like.

Her breath caught in her throat when she spotted the rectangular gap in the earth he'd been making. It looked like a grave. A body or a casket could fit into the space he'd dug.

# CHAPTER 3

*N*ext to the hole was the rock with the hand carved circle.

Scared, Faith looked around to make sure she was alone. As the evening darkened, she could see a quarter moon above and the treetops moving in the breeze. In the distance she could see an orange globe of light. She blinked and it was gone.

She rubbed her arms and looked for the light again in vain. What if he knew she was here? What if he knew she suspected foul play? It was all so eerie, she shivered and not because of the cold.

Still, she needed to investigate. After flipping on the flashlight, she squatted down and pointed it at the carving. On closer inspection, she now believed the smiley face was a sun with a line below it, like a rising sun. Under it, another sign was exposed now. It looked like a four-pointed star. The word evil settled in her mind as she noted other marks had been uncovered, but now she'd seen enough and wanted out of here.

As she stood, she heard branches snapping, like someone

was near. Roger's head moved back and forth, but he stayed at her side. She took a huge gulp of air and ran toward her house as fast as her legs could carry her. Roger followed closely behind.

Panting as much as Roger, she closed the front door behind her and turned the deadbolt. She felt safe now, and the first thing tomorrow she'd head to the Bureau of Land Management and look at records. For accuracy, she'd check out Brien's name and then she'd find a way to learn more about him. If he had any kind of record, she'd know.

THEY MET AT CITY HALL, Faith passing out as Brien passed in. She dressed professionally in a rose-colored pant suit and white high heels, looking tall and lean. Momentarily he wondered what kind of job she had that she had to dress so business-like. He didn't know what to say so he only nodded. She shot a quick smile in return.

The woman behind the desk was ready for him, which he didn't expect after living in the busy big city and waiting in many a line.

"You say you want to know who lives next to your claim, huh?"

"Yes, here is the address." He slid the piece of paper toward her.

The woman's eyebrows went up to hide in her bangs.

"Huh," she said, now squinting. "Did you ever think to ask your neighbor for their name?"

When he didn't answer, she took a page from her tablet and went to a back room. Moments later she handed the slip of paper to him. "Just as I thought."

Whatever that meant. "Uh … thank you."

"Huh," she said and turned away.

Did he say something wrong? he wondered.

"Casey and Faith Chadwick," he whispered to himself, while wondering where Casey went. Divorce maybe. At least he had a last name now.

Brien stopped in at the Murrayville Roadhouse. Every time he drove by cars flooded the parking lot, so he thought it must be the local hang out. From all appearances, breakfast time brought a lot of men to town to gather in the mornings.

The décor was country, with log banisters and rails. The chairs and tables were fashioned out of wood. Lanterns, an old horse harness and pictures of Murrayville's early gold mining history hung on the walls.

Brien sat down on a bar stool and swiveled to peruse the patrons. He didn't know a soul.

"Can I help you?" asked a petite woman with graying brown hair and a southern accent. A name tag clipped onto her pocket read *Lana* in bold letters.

"I'd like some black coffee, Lana. And the special."

After she jotted the order down, Brien tapped her wrist. "Say, you probably meet a lot of people working here."

"Well, you're right about that."

"Do you happen to know a woman named Faith Chadwick?"

"Yes, of course." After a moment Lana added, "Why she's the town mayor. Didn't you know that?"

Brien searched her face. She appeared serious enough. "I'm new around here."

"Yes, I figured that."

Stunned, Brien took more than a moment to process Lana's words while she moved toward the kitchen.

"I said, your coffee is ready, sir," Lana said to Brien.

He burned his tongue on the first gulp and told himself to start focusing.

~

FAITH GAZED out the detective's window. The grounds were scattered with magnificent red, white and blue petunias. Yet, right now it was hard to concentrate on anything but the information she'd just received from her good friend, Holly Mason.

Elbow on desk, Holly leaned forward and put her other hand to the back of her short brown hair. "Brien McGrew has never been in trouble with the law. He did get a ticket in 2015 for blocking an intersection. Should I bring him in?"

Holly snapped her gum, obviously waiting for the humor to reach Faith's ears.

"What does he do?"

"No current employer."

She pointed her finger at Holly. "Ah, ha!"

"Wait just a minute; there are lots of good people who don't have a job."

"Yeah, maybe that's why he's mining for gold."

"How can you take an instant dislike for this man when you've only just met him?"

"You've told me before not to be so trusting."

"Yeah, well this one's different."

Faith crossed her arms. "For Pete's sake, how do you know that?"

"Are you ready?" Holly gave her a full lopsided grin.

"Of course, I'm ready."

"He just graduated from Pepperdine Law School."

"An attorney," she said more to herself than to Holly.

"Yes, and he's had offers from two big firms. Want to know which ones?"

"No." After a moment, she said. "How did you find this out anyway?"

"Have you stopped watching detective shows on TV? We

have ways of making people talk." Holly laughed, but Faith looked at her through squinting eyes.

"What is it about this man, Faith?"

"Nothing. I don't want to talk about him anymore," she said, and left Holly's office to peals of laughter.

Faith wanted him to be a crook to explain why he did strange things next door. Maybe more important, to make her not want to be attracted to him, so she'd not put herself in the same predicament she got herself in before. Twice.

She tried to relax and look at the summer beauty around her. Now, if Holly thought Brien was harmless, then shouldn't she? But serial killer Ted Bundy went to law school, too, she reminded herself, walking back to work.

BRIEN LEVELED his trailer on the gravel pad and put two wood blocks behind the tires to make sure it wasn't going anywhere.

At the motel he'd occupied, he was able to take the hose and fill the trailer with enough water for a time and with a twist of a hand the propane was ready to use.

From the truck, he grabbed all the plastic bags full of groceries he could handle and took them inside. He took in a breath through his nose. His gently used trailer still smelled new.

After placing the bags on the table and counter, he filled the refrigerator with perishable contents. Now he was settled in for a while until he needed propane, water or pumping services.

He liked the trailer a lot because it included a toy hauler for his four-wheeler, and planned to keep it after his adventure was over. Who knows, maybe he'd even come back during vacation from the big city. This reminded him that he still hadn't decided which job to take.

To clearly align his goals, he'd hoped for insight and thought getting back to nature would bring him closer to God, as it had for Pops. Now that he'd settled, he had nothing else to fret about and could think as he worked the ground.

Well, there was one other problem, the town mayor. If she had a clue about what he was doing, she could expose it to the whole town if she wanted. This was his find and his find only. No, his presence here had to be kept quiet. Perhaps he could distract her.

Brien stepped out and stood before the marked boulders. How grateful he was that the evergreen bush he helped his grandfather plant in front of the rock, remained and flourished. He'd always hoped the thought of buried gold could be true but as he grew older, he found the thought a childish fantasy. Sure, his grandfather had a letter from his great-great grandfather explaining where to find the hidden Harney County gold, but why hadn't any of the earlier generations found it? It seemed almost impossible that they could be so lucky with only a few clues and a totally different environment not suitable to an earlier era. Yet, he somehow needed to be here again, with or without gold, and he had God to thank for finding this site again.

He heard a vehicle in the distance. Through the bush he could see Faith arriving home. Not long after, he could hear the click of her heals on the driveway as she went to get her mail. Obviously, she took hard steps to be heard from this distance.

With mail in hand, her chin was up, her eyes were on her house and he hoped she purposely avoided him.

Kind of. It surprised him to find that she'd damaged his male pride a bit.

Before he turned, he saw Roger running around the front yard, ears flapping and smiled.

Out of the corner of her eye, Faith could see that her new neighbor had moved in. Not for the first time did she wonder why he wanted to be so close to her home. Couldn't he have parked the trailer to the very furthest edge of his claim? The BLM told her he had forty acres.

Faith could only imagine what would happen to that cute little trailer if he started blasting again. Only her problem if it came too close to home.

It was good of Holly to look this guy up. She was a good friend and rarely did this sort of thing, she knew. Faith reminded herself for the tenth time that Holly wasn't worried, so why should she care? Maybe because he dug a grave beneath some sort of crazy rock cravings. A dedication to a god, perhaps?

Trying not to look out her side window, she flipped through the mail. After placing a few bills in a basket, she went to the bedroom to slip on flats.

Looking around, she could see the windows were intact and set out for the backyard. Still not looking Brien's way, she, and Roger, moved a sprinkler and turned it on.

There were other reasons to avoid Brien, she knew. Recently, she'd dated a man only one time, and the town nearly had them married off in a fortnight. It was embarrassing, humiliating, and he found a job out of town.

When she ran for mayor, she had no idea she'd become the town's heroine. It was cute at first, the attention and support, but she wanted nothing more than to help the town move forward. Suddenly people knew her whereabouts as soon as she did, and it became downright spooky.

She chuckled out loud. As if he'd be interested in her. Brien showed no inclination whatsoever. Still, Faith sat on her back-porch steps thinking about her neighbor until she needed to move the sprinkler.

An old red truck moved slowly down the road. Her senses were on high alert since she and Brien were the only ones out here. Further, Brien's trailer was back, hidden behind brush and trees. It probably looked to most people like the trailer belonged to her place, if visible.

From a safe corner of her house, she watched as the man cruised by slowly and lingered for a moment on the road opposite Brien's claim. She didn't recognize the truck, or the man, because his head was partially hidden with a cap and he kept his head low.

She wondered if he could see Brien. Great. Just great. People will know soon, and it will all begin again.

Brien stood behind a tree watching Faith bend over to change the sprinkler. Not that he was a voyeur, he just looked over and her skirt inched up her legs.

The sound of a vehicle made him jump, and he moved further back, out of sight from the road. He could see that Roger was barking from the front yard but stopped as the truck moved on.

Except for the partial road of crushed rock that was visible, his trailer was out of the line of sight. So, unless he pulled in and tried to find him, he wouldn't see anything. Even if he did, he'd probably chock it up to a camper that belonged to Faith.

He wondered if Faith had told anyone that he was here. He'd told her he wanted privacy and hopefully she'd obliged. It didn't hurt to remind her, he guessed.

Once the truck turned around and moved past, Brien went to the front of Faith's house as she had headed inside.

"Hello, Brien," she said, but her tone belied the pleasantry. Roger came out the screen door to welcome him.

"Hello, Faith." He patted Roger's head and then stomped his feet on the door mat. "Can I speak to you for a moment?"

"Sure."

Faith nearly pushed him inside, then looked both ways out front before she closed the door.

Her feet were bare; she'd kicked off her shoes and now bent to push them out of the way. Her rear end was in his line of vision again, closer this time.

She turned and arched a perfectly shaped eyebrow.

He shook his head, trying to remember why he came over. "I want my time here to be private," he said.

"I figured as much."

He nodded. "Okay. Have you told anyone that I'm living here?"

"Only my detective friend, but I doubt she has plans of talking to anyone about it. She has a life."

"Humph."

She crossed her arms. "Does that bother you? Do you have something to hide?"

"Well, no. I want to be left alone, is all."

"Suits me, too. I want my life to be private as well," she said with a nod of her head. "Can you leave out the back door, please?"

He nodded and she walked him through the house to the back door, making him feel like a chastened child. If he wasn't mistaken, she was ashamed of him being anywhere near her.

Well, this was what he was after, wasn't it? It was fine with him. He sighed several times as he made his way through the trees and brush to his trailer.

Brien said he didn't have anything to hide, so she should just march right over there and ask him what he was really doing.

From her bedroom window she tried to spot Brien

through the brush. She caught a glimpse of him stretching his arms crisscross around himself, then straight up. No doubt he felt muscle strain after all the digging.

Whoops. She backed away from the window. He'd looked over and almost caught her staring his way.

Could it be possible that he'd grown more attractive since she last saw him? No, it was probably her hormones bouncing around. When one was hungry, food looked especially good. It had to be the same thing for her with Brien.

Suddenly it all made sense to her. She wanted Brien's attention even though she feared the consequences. She feared wanting Brien, not getting enough of him, and then it would be obvious to everyone that they were together, and she'd turn into the town's obsession once again. She knew by experience that it was hard to keep a boyfriend under those circumstances.

After shaking her head as if to clear it, she chuckled at herself for stressing over something so one-sided. "Get real, Chadwick."

# CHAPTER 4

*S*aturday morning Faith slept in until eight o'clock. After a leisurely bubble bath, she pulled on jean shorts and a pink shell. Then she stood next to her bedroom window and looked for signs of Brien.

After a huge sigh, she decided to tear her eyes away from the man and think about breakfast. No, the pantry, she'd organize the pantry, she thought nervously. It was long overdue.

Before she could change her mind, she emptied two shelves and started to categorize the items. But Roger started getting into the foodstuffs, so she let him outside. Organizing didn't take as long as she thought, so afterwards she went to her office area to purge files.

Okay, so she felt good about getting some things done. Yet, her wandering mind didn't let her appreciate it for long. If she didn't forget about Brien, she'd have her whole house organized in alphabetical order by the end of the day. As good as that could be, it wasn't the kind of weekend she wanted.

The silence was deafening, so she wondered about Roger.

On the back porch, she whistled with two fingers, but he didn't return. That troubled her because he nearly always came when she whistled. She waited a moment and then stepped out of her sandals and into her boots and headed in the direction of Brien's. On closer inspection, she found him shoveling along the edge of the rock then stooping to sweep with a whisk broom. Roger was below sniffing and digging himself. No wonder he didn't hear her. Traitor.

"Hello," she called, far enough away not to startle Brien.

He looked toward the street and turned to her with a frown.

She couldn't remember anyone so insolent to her, even during election time. There's a strike against him.

"Yes?"

"I was looking for my dog." Roger leapt to her side and ran a dirty paw down her leg. She steadied her hand on Roger's head and he sat down beside her.

"I hope he wasn't bothering you."

"No, as a matter-of-fact he was helping me." He directed a smile down to Roger. A smile she sure didn't get.

"Cute trailer."

He squinted at her rather apprehensively. "Thanks. I like it."

"The ground's rocky, isn't it?"

"Yes, it is." He looked down at his watch.

He didn't want to talk, it was evident, but she wasn't done yet.

"I heard you're a graduate."

With furrowed brow, he said, "How did you know that?"

"I have a detective friend, remember?"

"Is it legal to have someone checked out like that?"

"I don't really know. You're the attorney."

"Humph."

"Hey, I was a little concerned about my neighbor digging a hole that looked like a grave." There she said it.

He smiled, then chuckled. After a moment, he said. "Does that scare you?"

"My friend told me I shouldn't be afraid of you. I'm not so sure."

He smiled again, fuller this time. He had a dimple in his cheek. Obviously, he hadn't smiled enough for her to notice it before.

She put a hand on her hip. "I think you're making some sort of shrine to the sun god."

"Oh, yeah?"

"Sure. Stand back over here by me and look at it from my perspective."

"All right."

He stood in her personal space and she could smell his aftershave. *Nice.*

"I see what you mean," he said, and crossed his arms. She enjoyed looking at an occasional flexing muscle but turned away anyway.

"What is the sun god anyway?" she asked.

"A deity that represents the sun, I guess. I do know that the Chinese, Hindus and Egyptians have had sun gods."

"And what do you put on the altar to sacrifice?" she said with a smile.

She was so darn cute, talking about sun gods. He couldn't wait to hear what else she had to say.

"A virgin," he said.

"Why does it always have to be a virgin woman, why can't it be a virgin man?"

"Now that's a good question. Maybe you can look that up online."

"No, we know the culture, we know the answer."

"Now wait a minute, you're not a man and I heard you're the town mayor."

She nodded. "I think it's because my name is Faith. Who could disagree with posters that said, 'Keep the Faith,' or 'Have Faith in your town?'"

"Think so, huh?"

"Well, they also didn't particularly want the retired chief of police either." She sat on a boulder and pulled her knees to her chin. "Whatever the reason, I truly wanted to do this job. I'm right where I want to be."

"Huh. Political aspirations."

"Maybe even beyond Murrayville, we'll see."

"What makes you the right candidate?"

"Good question, Brien. I can work with people, I guess. I learned about behaviors teaching middle school and, truly, isn't politics all about behaviors these days?"

"Very admirable ambitions, I'd say, even though that's an unusual political comparison."

She gave him a wide smile, half humor and half proud, he'd say.

They sat in silence looking out at the nice June day.

"Well, McGrew, where's the rainbow?"

"I beg your pardon?"

She stood and looked from one edge of the sky to the other.

Perhaps they had come to some sort of truce.

"You're Irish, Brien McGrew. You must be looking for your

pot of gold at the end of the rainbow."

Brien's head fell back with laughter. "You've found me out."

She didn't smile, but her eyes twinkled.

"Ah, that's a good one. That's good."

She smiled then. "Tell me about yourself, Brien McGrew."

"What do you want to know?"

"Start at the beginning, of course."

"Born in Portland. Have an older sister. In high school, I got interested in the debate team and went to state. Just graduated from law school."

"Nice. Congrats. What brought you here?"

"My grandfather. He loved this area and took me camping often."

Faith heard a car approaching. At the same time, they jumped up and Faith hid behind a bush, Brien a tree. She peeked out and saw a gray car pull into her driveway. As fast as her feet could take her, she rushed to her backyard and then in the back door.

CHAPTER 5

$\mathcal{M}$ona Sprague stopped by; she did from time to time. They'd been friends ever since they started working together as English teachers at Murrayville Middle School. She knocked at the door at the same time Faith entered the back of the house.

"H-e-l-l-o, Mona."

"Hi. Have you been jogging or something?"

Faith put a hand to her forehead, looked behind to the partially opened back door and said, "I was in the back, heard you pull up and rushed in."

"Sounds like you're more out of shape than I am."

She had to smile because Mona was sixty and she'd told her one time that she had fifty pounds to lose.

Mona chuckled and handed her a plastic grocery bag. "I have some extra flower seeds. Thought you could use them, and it's a good excuse to come see you. I know it must be lonely out here."

Mona plopped down on a chair. "Bob's watching his favorite show on TV. It's too violent for me so I thought I'd come visit."

"Well, thanks for the seeds and for thinking of me, but you know I don't mind being by myself."

"That's what you always say." Mona looked at her through squinting eyes.

Faith nodded but knew what was coming. One, two, three-

"Jerry, from the business office, is still interested in you."

"He's interested in anything that wears a skirt. Haven't you noticed him ogling every woman that passes him?"

"That's because he's a lonely man. Needs a woman."

"Huh."

"Aren't you even interested in men?"

"Well, of course. If you're saying... Don't be starting rumors."

Mona waved a hand. "Oh, settle down, I'm not saying anything like that, but do you even know what you want in a relationship?"

What was it about her that everyone wanted to see her married? Faith knew that Mona cared about her, believed she'd be happier with a man, but obviously the time was not at hand for her. "Yes, but right now I stand just fine on my own."

Mona looked toward the kitchen. "Do you have any of your specially blended iced tea?"

"Sure, I'll have some, too."

Mona followed her into the kitchen. "Okay, so what's your ideal man like?"

Faith grabbed two glasses and started to fill them with ice. "Maybe dark hair and brown eyes." She turned to get the pitcher of tea from the refrigerator. "Firm square jaw. Broad shoulders. Levi's and black t-shirt."

"You act like you already know this person. Who is it?"

Faith almost dropped the glass of iced tea she was in the middle of handing to her.

"Oh, uh…"

"He sounds wonderful, who is he? Come on, spit it out."

Oh, *no.* "How about the latest James Bond."

"Oh, Faith, you had me going."

"He has a dimple in one of his cheeks, right?"

Mona put a hand on her hip. "I'm not sure, but I don't think he has dark brown hair. I'm thinking I better take a closer look around town."

Faith realized she'd made a mistake describing Brien. Inwardly she sighed, not believing she'd given a description of Brien to Mona. Yet, it just came out unbidden, probably because their last meeting ended so well that it gave her a little thrill.

If Mona ran into him, she'd know right away who Faith's ideal man happened to be. Until then, she'd better stop in town and buy a James Bond movie or two and place them strategically around the house.

"How are your classes going, Mona?"

Mona swallowed a sip of tea and said, "Pretty well, but there's some more bullying going on at school."

"Oh?"

"Well, you know there's always some we miss, but this time it was serious. Lawsuit serious."

"Anybody I know?"

"Probably not, he's new and I didn't see your name on the bully's class schedule. As soon as the threat of a lawsuit hit the air, the family disappeared. They were vagabonds anyway, so it wasn't much of a problem to them, I suppose."

"Bullying seems to be in epidemic proportions, if you listen to the media anyway. It not only takes place at school, but in churches, families, the workplace, at home and in neighborhoods."

"Yep. Don't know what else we can do," said Mona with a frown and a tap of her foot.

They sat in silence for a few moments then, Faith sat up straight. "Same here. Don't know. We can't help the kids if we can't help ourselves. Take politics for example…need I say more?"

"Nope got it completely. How's your classes going?" asked Mona.

"I must say it's wonderful only working the afternoon, three classes one day and two the next. Even with my morning work as mayor, teaching is a nice diversion and I can concentrate a bit more on the fewer students."

"I must say I envy your having fewer classes," Mona said with a wistful sigh.

"Yes, but you have more money coming in. Thankfully Dad's investment in real estate earlier on helped pay for this house. That's why I can do it."

They both took a few sips of tea. Faith said, "I have maybe two weeks to apply for grant money for the town. I have no idea what to present."

"What? Then you'd better get at it."

"But still, no matter how great the project and submission, grants do not always go through. I'm telling myself that, as much as to you, Mona."

An hour later, Faith watched Mona leave from her front window. At least her eyes were directed that way. Her mind lingered on her visit with Brien.

Whoa, Faith, whoa. Out her side window she saw Brien hide behind a tree when Mona drove by. Sorry, detective Holly, he isn't guilt free. If possible, she was even more dedicated to finding out what was behind his actions. She was the mayor of this town and she needed to know.

BRIEN WATCHED Faith's visitor drive down the road. Probably

a friend of hers, he decided. Yet, Faith wasn't expecting anyone, he knew, because she hid behind the bushes as soon as she heard the oncoming car. Who could Faith be hiding from? he wondered. An old boyfriend, an ex-husband? She seemed quick to run, so it had to be something serious.

Faith wasn't shy about saying she wanted to be alone out here. He wondered if she could be doing something illegal. Yet, he didn't notice anyone suspicious going to and from her house.

Whatever it was, he was determined to find out why she's behaving this way.

He couldn't get her off his mind, and it was not just her actions he thought about, which was not the smartest turn of his attention.

Sunday, the following day, Brien got up early and watched the sun rise through the treetops. He hadn't been to church in a while, but he remembered his grandfather's admonition to look for God no matter where you were. At the thought of Pops, he put his hands over his face and tried to see him in his mind's eye. Words that he'd heard Pops spout while camping in the past floated through his consciousness.

*"Out here in the wilderness, a man can find God. You relax and calm down enough to listen, gaining inspiration from the Almighty through the wind, mountains, and streams. If you're seeking, thoughts will come that will give you a path to follow and goals to commit to. Not a better place than this to get close to God."*

Brien was doing that just now. Thinking about his future and which job offer to take. Out here, in the peacefulness, neither job seemed right to him. However, there were no better offers out there than what he'd received. He wondered what his grandfather would think about them. He looked away from the light of the sunrise then, and from the momentary glimpse at God.

Instead, he turned and watched Faith's house and the little telltale signs that she was up and moving around. He looked away when her bedroom shade went up.

He turned back toward the sunrise and the treetops gently swaying in the breeze. He felt his thoughts lighten, glad he was here as a reward for working so hard to graduate from law school and then preparation for the bar.

One of happiest moments in his life so far had been passing the bar in Oregon. Another was being here, right here, with Pops camping and dreaming of the gold they'd come back and find. But the years flew by and then Pops died. He was so young and foolish to think that Pops would be around forever, that they'd have a chance to find the gold together anytime he wanted to.

This place was their secret. He'd not told anyone, and he didn't think Pops did either. He wished now he would have thought to spread his ashes out here, but, sadly, he was too busy thinking about his future to stop and realize anything important until now.

"Sorry, Pops, I didn't get back here with you." The wind pushing along some small pinecones was the only answer he received.

He stood and turned toward the hole he'd made. Again, time would not stand still for him, so he'd best keep moving.

WHAT COULD BE BETTER than to get out in nature? Faith believed a walk or jog through the forest was a regenerating thing. A time to breathe in the pine scented air and reflect on the Creator. She had a lot of blessings and a lot to be thankful for. The day was beautiful, promising a high of eighty degrees. Now at eleven o'clock, it was well on its way.

She'd not run in the direction of her new neighbor, as

Roger had, but follow a deer trail into the forest. Surely, he'd catch up with her soon.

Faith stopped when she spotted a murder of crows filling the limbs of a deciduous tree. The flapping of wings stopped, and then nothing, they were silent.

She wondered why a group of crows were called murder, as the name wouldn't endear them to anyone. Goosebumps formed on her arms.

A pebble hit her in the thigh, stinging her. She scanned the area behind her while startled crows squawked and flew out and around her.

The angle of the sting told her it must have been shot from the brush. It was hard to turn her eyes from the squawking birds, but she did, while saying a Bible verse she learned during her youth, "Perfect love cast out all fear."

She could have called out, but the worry of getting an answer motivated her on to break her high school track record. After some minutes, and no one followed, she slowed enough to jog at her regular pace. The crows certainly weren't startled by the pebble cast at her and she had slowed down, posing no threat. She wondered why a hiker would want to throw a rock at her; certainly, a woman jogger posed no problem for anyone.

Could Brien be that twisted that he would head back to the thick of the forest just to give her a start? She didn't think so. Besides, Roger would follow him if he had.

MARTY WALKER TOOK a sigh of relief and then chuckled to himself. He was so close, so close. Not that he planned on Faith jogging right to him. No, he'd been hiking around the area learning the trails that lead to Faith's house.

He took another breath and felt joy within after seeing

her again, and then touching her. He'd touched her with a small rock, but he touched her, nonetheless.

After watching the muscles of her lower body move in unison, and her breast moving with their own rhythm, he didn't want her to stop. He only wanted to reach out to her in some way, but not to be caught.

Faith had come across to him as a strong woman, someone who would have called out and found an answer to who would strike out at her. But she didn't, she had a weak spot. He looked forward to taking this information home and mulling it over.

He looked up to the sky. The crows had moved on and with them, his girl. It was enough for today.

"WHAT ARE YOU DOING?" Faith asked Brien. His back went ramrod straight. She'd startled him, but that was not her intent.

Brien took a deep breath and after a moment said, "Top of the morning to ya, Faith."

He'd used an Irish accent and she couldn't help but chuckle and try to imitate. "Aye, McGrew."

He still didn't answer her, she noticed. Didn't seem to plan to, just stared out toward the road, then her.

Didn't look like they'd share a friendly conversation like they had not so long ago. Yet, better to try and make friends with the enemy, she thought. "Want some breakfast?" she asked. "I have some pancakes ready to put on the grill."

Brien's jaw dropped and then his eyebrows went up.

"No need to look so shocked, I only asked you to a neighborly breakfast. Pepper bacon was on sale, okay?"

He smiled. "Yes, breakfast would be nice. I'm hungry."

"Good." She waved her arm. "Come on."

She heard him following behind, with Roger dancing around him. An arm reached around her to open the screen door.

"It is a beautiful morning," he said.

"Yes, every day I appreciate living out here." She put the bacon on her portable grill and set the lid down. "I guess I prefer forests with juniper, pines and firs better than the rain forest with more underbrush."

Brien took an oak chair, turned it backward and placed his arms along the top of the back. "Yes, it's a different kind of forest here than in the Portland area."

"Don't get me wrong, I think Portland is beautiful, especially for a large town," she said.

"Yes, it is, and quite different from Malibu where I finished law school."

"Not much winter there, I imagine."

Brien shook his head. "Don't really need a winter coat in Malibu."

After pouring pancakes onto a pan, she turned and said, "Must be nice, gets pretty cold here in the winter."

"Yeah, it was nice, but I never wanted to live there on a long-term basis."

Faith took a pitcher of orange juice from the refrigerator and set it on the counter. "I suppose you won't see our cold winter here."

"I'm not quite sure yet."

Faith filled two small glasses with orange juice and moved to turn the bacon. "By then you'll have had your fill of cold weather."

After a moment of silence, he said, "Ask me about it later on."

"Isn't it a good thing to have a plan?"

Brien's eyes widened, obviously he didn't like what she'd

said. He stood and turned to look out the window at the back of her property.

"Did I say something wrong?"

"I'm not a slacker, Faith, it's just my life has been planned out for so long, it seems good to take a pause, yet strange not knowing my future in entirety."

According to Holly, he had two good job offers; she wondered why he didn't snap one up. Faith motioned for Brien to sit back down. "I suppose it's a bad time to look for work, too. In this economy."

"I may have some time."

"Eat up."

"I will."

She wondered if he wanted to be a slacker after all. Not that it mattered to her. Or, maybe he was trying to work through something, and it had everything to do with digging next door.

He ate quietly, as if preoccupied. "I need to get going, I have a lot to do today."

Brien turned at the door and smiled. "Thanks for the food and the company."

"Certainly."

## CHAPTER 6

Faith had dreamed of being a mayor, like her father, since she was ten years old. Now, she held the office while he was a free bird, a retired schoolteacher following a trail from Oregon to Arizona.

Yet that was okay. She'd gotten stronger by handling the town's problems on her own. Yes, early on she'd gained the respect of the town, and she'd done that by being active in the town's politics and by being a darn good middle school teacher. Her students passed the state tests, and she'd worked very hard to make that happen.

Not for the first time did she wonder why she didn't just stay where she was. If she could make students at such an awkward age learn, then shouldn't teaching be her true calling?

Perhaps her childhood dream got in the way of what she should do with her life. No, she wasn't sure that she was off track with her calling. Even though she didn't have a diehard agenda, she had hopes for the town.

Faith only wanted privacy in return, but apparently for the town mayor it had been too much to ask.

If anything, the town had lost respect for her as the months passed. Twice, she became fodder for wagging tongues, with boyfriends Andy and Mark, two men she'd grown to love in the last two years. They were swept away, out of town to be precise, due to the beady eyes that followed their every move.

Her morals were questioned, when if anything, she'd been more respectable as a mayor. She attended church with the best of them and did it because she'd always gone; being a mayor didn't make her feel any differently about God. As a matter of fact, she needed His guidance even more.

She wished she didn't care so much about what people thought. Then again, how did she become such a people pleaser? Maybe it wouldn't matter if the men she'd hoped to spend her life with had the guts to stick around.

And it hurt, by golly. Was it too much to ask to be loved by a man through thick and thin?

Brien represented a devilish temptation, but even though a handsome guy, she didn't need to go through the kind of personal loss and pain she went through before. Instead of choosing and taking a job offer, he'd apparently rather dig for fairytale treasure. She couldn't explain what he was doing in any other way. She seemed to be attracted to the same type of guy, which frightened her to no end.

Now, thinking about the two men she'd thought she'd come close to marrying, she felt nothing. Her heart seemed to have closed off or hardened somehow.

This town, Murrayville, she continued to love. All the people, young and old, stated in so many words how proud they were of her when she was elected. At first, no man appeared to be good enough for her. Perhaps they'd done her a favor chasing the men off.

~

Step one, go to school. Step two, graduate. Step three, spend a summer with Pops looking for gold. Step four, settle down at that dream job he'd worked so hard for.

The trouble was that he couldn't even think about step four, still stuck in step three.

How he missed Pops. If Brien had known he was going to die, he'd have taken a hiatus from school. He'd just died so quickly, after being diagnosed with pancreatic cancer.

So, here he was alone. Still, he felt his presence at times or perhaps it was just that he thought about him nearly every waking moment.

Together they had studied signs pointed to Spanish treasure, even though the Harney County gold was probably buried without signs since no one in the family had found it. Pops just said they needed to be prepared.

Now Brien wondered precisely where Pops would've started to dig? What did he think the signs meant? Oh, how Pops would have loved to have seen these other signs carved into rock so very long ago.

After Pops died, Brien had studied everything he could get his hands on about buried treasure, and the signs people carved centuries before to help them, or a cohort, to retrieve the cache later. Now he had new information that Pops didn't. Someday, on the other side, he'd meet Pops again and tell him all about it.

An old red pickup came down the road, slowly. Brien was pretty sure that it was the same pickup he'd seen driving by before.

This time he tried to get a look at the driver, but a high collar, sunglasses, and a low cap kept the guy incognito, especially at a distance. The man looked ahead, and only inched by Faith's place. Brien had seen Faith in her backyard, so he stepped through the brush and trees to get a closer look.

Faith turned from the house and stealthily moved toward

the bushes herself. Nearing him, she looked up with wide eyes and an intake of air. However shocked at his presence, she still moved until she was out of the way of anyone trying to find her.

"Hello, Brien," she said, with a smile and a hand on her chest, as if attempting to avoid a caller was an everyday occurrence, and certainly not anything to be concerned about.

"Hello," he said and continued to watch her. She bent down as if to pick up a pinecone, when in fact she moved her body down and away.

Brien slipped behind a tree.

"Say, are you hiding from someone?" he asked, concerned.

She put a hand to her chest and smiled a smile that didn't reach her eyes. "Me?"

"Well, I'm not talking to the squirrel up there."

She followed the direction of his gaze and squinted, no doubt spotting the dark, scrawny looking squirrel above.

"I don't know who that is," she said, pointing her thumb behind her.

"Still, you walked away."

"Yes," she said, nonchalantly, like it didn't matter in the least.

"He doesn't appear to be stopping anyway," he added.

She didn't answer, only made sure she was out of view of the truck that made a U-turn and was now driving away.

"I can't help but notice you're hiding from this man."

"Or woman."

She was right; it was hard to say for sure at this distance.

"Could be he, or she, was looking for you, Brien."

"I'm not expecting anyone."

Brien's eyes widened when she made that statement, making Faith think that she was not far from the truth.

"An unrequited love perhaps?" she asked with a smile.

"No, I don't think so, that is unless you are referring to yourself."

"No, no. Not me."

He looked back in the direction the truck had taken. "He doesn't appear to be coming back."

"Yep. Just the way I like it."

"Me, too."

Faith crossed her arms, waiting for him to address the unrequited love topic. His lips thinned. Not going there.

"If I had my way, I'd have a roadblock put in."

"You're the mayor, can't you do that?" he said with a wink.

"If I did that, I'd have a stream of visitors with cameras at the ready."

"Small town life doesn't suit you, huh?"

She thought for a moment. "I like it here."

"I'm not convinced. On a scale of one to ten, ten being love and one being hate, how would you rate it?"

"You're not working for the newspaper, are you?"

Brien crossed his arms, too. "No, I'm an attorney."

He said the word attorney and then looked down and smiled, like the word was new to his lips and he liked the sound of it rolling across his tongue. She smiled, understanding his accomplishment.

"I rate it eight-point-five."

"And the one-point-five?"

"My private life."

"Hmmm."

"What's that supposed to mean?"

"I don't see much of a private life." He shrugged. "After work you're home most of the time. You had a friend in to chat. Looks like you like to do a little gardening. You love your dog."

Roger walked by at that moment and headed toward the "hole."

She desperately wanted him to take back the words about her private life. Who was he anyway, that she had to spill her guts to him? She looked down and realized she'd been tapping her foot.

"So, no, I guess I don't understand what you mean by the one-point-five that you don't like."

She could tell he tried to keep a straight face, but then he burst out laughing.

With pointed finger, she said, "Humor is great, but I don't like it at my expense."

He stuck his hands in his pockets, took a deep breath and sobered. "I'm sorry. Didn't mean to hurt your feelings."

"You didn't hurt my feelings, you made me mad."

"I stand corrected."

"Humph. I suppose you're taking a vacation from every-thing including your private life."

"Pretty much, yes."

That was all there was to it, she'd just stop right there. Losing two men she'd deeply cared about was not funny. "Looks like you're taking a break from...from whatever it is you're doing here," she said, waving a hand.

"Yes, the excitement in the neighborhood distracted me somehow."

"Humph."

Brien gave her an ear-to-ear smile.

"I'll go a...tend to my garden before the day heats up."

Halfway back, she turned and caught him watching her. She gave her best imitation of a wiggle-walk, not expecting the chuckle she heard from him in the distance.

"Humph," she repeated, annoyed.

∾

FAITH CAME HOME FROM WORK, let Roger out for a while then headed back to town to eat at Murrayville Roadhouse.

She'd avoided coming home after eating because she dreaded going home to an empty house. Besides what good was changing the town, if no one was around to share it with?

No doubt, she'd been fine these months before Brien came around. After a busy day, she thought she'd be too tired to feel anything. Even after mingling with the people of town she didn't fill that void, so after seven o'clock she headed home.

Faith grabbed her laptop computer and sat down with Roger laying on her feet. Social media and reading emails helped some, so she stayed in her chair until the sun went down, and she needed to turn on a light.

Instead, Faith stood at the window looking for Brien's lighted trailer in the distance. She saw fire light and a glimpse of Brien sitting alongside when the flame hit just right.

She enjoyed a good fire and wanted to join him. She considered it a moment, then went to the kitchen and made two hot chocolates. She poured them into two covered coffee mugs.

Faith stuck a small flashlight in her mouth, picked up the two hot chocolates and pushed the screen door open with her behind.

She hoped she wouldn't scare Brien, but she couldn't very well call out to him with her mouth full. He looked startled, a little, when she called out, "Hewoo!"

Thankfully, she saw recognition in his eyes as he stood up. "Hewoo to you, too."

He moved his lawn chair closer to her. "Let me take that."

She handed him a hot chocolate, but he reached for the flashlight.

"Oh, thanks. Sorry about the spit."

"I'm thinking this drink may make up for it."

"Hot chocolate. I threw in a few marshmallows for good measure."

"Sounds good. Thanks."

"I'm sorry to bother you, but I saw the fire and I just had to come and enjoy the ambience."

"Here, take my chair. Scoot up to the fire."

"I think I will."

He didn't really have to tell her that as she'd already gravitated to the heat. After sitting on a rock, he opened the lid and took a small sip.

This was a nice surprise. The evenings were lonely, and he'd been thinking about Faith and then she'd appeared.

"Found any gold?" Her smile was ear-to-ear.

"You know I did take some dirt down to the closest creek I could find. Found a few flakes. This is good. I appreciate the marshmallows."

"Welcome." After another sip, she added, "I've heard there's flakes of gold everywhere from John Day to the Boise Basin."

"That's what Pops believed."

"Pops?"

"Grandfather. He passed away some months back."

"I'm sorry to hear that." She said, trying to give him eye contact but he turned away.

"Thanks. We were very close."

"When my mom died the words, meet you on the other side, had real meaning for me."

"That is my hope, too. To see him on the other side."

"Oh. I see a bat flying by."

He saw it too, at the edge of the far-reaching light of the fire. "Are you frightened?"

"No. I've seen them before. They don't seem to be interested in me." After a moment of silence, she said, "I did see a bunch of crows the other day. A murder of crows. Now that spooked me."

"Crows don't bother me at all."

"They don't usually bother me either, but when I was jogging, a whole group of them flew into the top of a large tree and were absolutely silent. It was the strangest thing."

"I know what that means, I think. According to a nature show I watched, it means that a crow has died, and they are giving some sort of tribute to it."

Faith tipped her head toward him and he could see narrowing eyes from the light of the fire. "What?"

He chuckled. "I am telling the truth, at least as well as I know it. Like I said, I heard this explained on a show."

"Huh, and I got to actually see it. Smart birds."

"So, they say."

"They started flying off and it felt like someone threw a pebble at my leg."

"Really? Do you think a pebble flew from the commotion?"

She shook her head. "It came from a different way. It didn't fall from anywhere. So, I took off running toward home."

"Hey, are we telling ghost stories here? Good setting for it, I guess."

She was quiet for a minute, making him think that she still struggled with what had happened to her. Not surprising. A murder of crows filling a tree and not making a sound could freak out anyone.

"I'm going to apply for a grant," she finally said.

"Impressive."

"I want to put this place on the map. I want Oregon to know about us."

"Impressive."

"It's just I want so much for this town," she said, as if he didn't mean his words.

"I really mean it. Impressive. You're doing a lot at your young age."

He caught a flash of white teeth.

"And what about you? You've accomplished a lot in your years, too."

He rubbed his face. "It's just beginning, and I want to make decisions that matter." There he'd said it aloud. "Time alone has been making me think it seems."

"Being out here is the best place to be confused, because it's a good place to find answers. Close to nature, close to God, I think," Faith said.

"Yeah, that's what Pops always said. Not a better place to sort things out."

Faith sipped her cocoa and stared at the fire.

"I'm surprised you don't have a boyfriend coming around."

"Not a whole lot to choose from right now."

He smiled. "I used to say that I didn't have time and I truly didn't.

"And now?"

"And now I'm here for a while but going back to the big city to work. Not quite settled enough yet."

He stood up to poke and add wood to the fire. The fire burned, spit and lightened the area around them.

"Want your chair back? I can stand," she asked.

"No, I'm good. I'll stand for a while."

What a perfect night, Faith thought to herself. Here she sat in the light of a campfire with an interesting guy. His square chin had a golden glow to it and the dimple in his cheek flashed every so often.

"After mayor, then what?"

"Keep teaching middle school English."

"Your tone of voice tells me that would be okay."

"It would be okay; I enjoy teaching for the most part."

"But?"

"I always want to be open to what comes along in life. One door closes and another opens, so to speak. I don't believe much in coincidences, so I'm trying to pay attention."

"I don't think I could ever be that flexible."

She finished her last sip of cocoa in time for a breeze to blow smoke into her face, so she stood and put her back to the fire.

"So, you say you don't believe in coincidences."

"I suppose there are a few," she said turning her head to him.

"Then why are we together, here warming by the fire?"

"Good question, McGrew. I'm not totally sure yet, but I'm sure I can learn a lot from such a highly regarded attorney such as yourself."

"Touché."

It was a good time to leave, so she picked up the cups and headed back to the house with impatient Roger's nose, bumping the calf of her leg.

FAITH STRAIGHTENED her back and gazed at the Elkhorn Mountains in the distance. The beauties were topped with snow now, but it wouldn't be for long.

Soon her dad would be back from moving around the states and for a few weeks she could enjoy him. She knew that one of the reasons he'd left town was to give her space, and even if she appreciated it, her personal life didn't dictate privacy. Just ask neighbor Brien.

Brien. She'd asked him what he was up to two times before. The first time he said he was mining on his claim.

The second time she asked him, he looked down at the grave shaped hole and didn't answer. She wondered why she didn't put more strength or determination behind the questions that crossed her mind so often. Since when had she started succumbing to mere man? This should not be the practice of the mayor of Murrayville.

With early items from her garden and goods from the store, she'd make a nice crab salad for lunch and finally get to the bottom of this rock engraving business once and for all.

At noon Faith found Brien in the hole progressing so fast that she was sure he'd be in China before too long. At least she *thought* it was Brien. The man was covered with dirt from head to toe.

## CHAPTER 7

*R*oger looked down and barked.

"Don't get too close, you might fall in," Brien ordered Faith with an edge of breathlessness to his voice. He straightened and put a hand atop the shovel handle.

"I'll be careful. I'm here to invite you to lunch."

He smiled. "The offer is nice, but I'm pretty dirty right now."

"You can clean up. See you in an hour."

With a hand on Roger's collar, she pivoted, and, in a nanosecond, he couldn't see her from where he stood.

He'd planned on skipping lunch, working right through until dinner. But, if an attractive woman wanted him clean and at her house in an hour, he could hardly refuse.

Brien nicked himself shaving, something he hadn't done for a while, which made him think he was a bit preoccupied and nervous about seeing the mayor.

He wondered about that because he had a healthy self-esteem, especially by the time he made it to law school. But, he supposed, a good education is not all there is to feeling good about yourself. Feeling loved, he was sure, was another.

The last few minutes of waiting was murder. He should have been in the hole, because he'd paced enough to move another layer of dirt.

Faith sported a ponytail, tan Capris and a red golf shirt. Not fancy by any means, but he could see the lines of her figure as she moved about the kitchen.

She set a large bowl of salad on the table and smiled at him.

"Looks like crab."

"It is."

She grabbed a hot pad and pulled something wrapped in foil from the oven. It smelled like hot bread.

He wished he knew what to say instead of just standing there. "Need any help?"

"No, I got it. Want lemonade?"

"Please."

"Sit down. There is fine," she said and pointed. "You cleaned up nice."

"Thanks." He felt his face redden.

She handed him the bowl of salad and he spooned some onto his place. What was the matter with him? he wondered. Why couldn't he think of something to say? What would a woman want to talk about?

"I'm not sure what job to take." He sighed because he'd said it in an awkward tone, like he was needy or something.

"Need the mayor to help you figure it out?"

He suddenly felt like kissing the mayor. When he didn't answer right away, she said, "I could try."

Now he was sorry he brought the subject up. "Great salad."

"Thanks, I try to load it with goods."

"Cheese, bacon, boiled eggs. Love it."

"What kind of an attorney are you?" she asked between bites.

"Trial lawyer."

"Wow, *I'm* impressed," she said and moved her hand full of crispy bread toward her chest.

"Too many Perry Mason reruns as a kid," he said.

"I doubt that's the only reason."

"No, I originally wanted to help the innocent avoid a prison sentence."

"Not a bad goal."

He nodded. "The trouble is a young upstart can't always choose his clients."

Faith put her elbow on the table and her hand under her chin and looked at him as if studying his face. "You do know that trial lawyers don't always get the best rap?"

He set his fork down. "Certainly, but trial lawyers, for the most part, are the vindicators of our system of justice-including the, what would you say? Uh...strength of the First Amendment."

"I would think it would be hard to live with yourself if you free a guilty man. I'd sure want to choose my clients. That's just the mayor speaking."

He looked down at his plate then, with furrowed brow, and she wondered what he was thinking. After a moment, he said, "Whatever job I have, I will put my full effort into it." He put his napkin on his plate, clearly putting an end to this conversation.

"Looks like I'm scaring you off. Want some brownies for dessert?"

"Uh, yeah. Please."

Faith's words about choosing clients, twisted a knife somewhere deep inside his chest and he wished it were as easy as that. Even with choosing your clients, you could be wrong about character.

He watched her put a supersize brownie in a bowl and squeeze a bottle of Hershey's chocolate syrup in a circular motion over the top. After grabbing a tub of whipped cream from the refrigerator, she spooned a generous amount onto the concoction.

"Creative, I like that."

"No creative about it, this is the way I like it."

Brien helped her clear the dishes off the table. When they almost collided, he didn't step back but stopped and looked down at her lips instead.

"Do I have some chocolate on my mouth?"

"Wish you did. I love chocolate."

She put a hand up to push invisible hair toward her pony-tail and he slowly worked her hand into his.

It surprised him when something akin to electricity moved to the base of his stomach. When he could feel his heartbeat, he let her hand go then pulled back to see if she was ready for a kiss.

Her eyes looked startled for a second before she let out an almost silent gasp. He believed she felt it, too. He was very curious about what those lips felt like, yet now wasn't the right time. Maybe they'd never have a right time. With all the power he could muster, he took a seat again.

She took a deep breath and closed her eyes. When they opened her eyebrows bunched up. "Tell me. What do the symbols on the rocks mean?"

A woman could be a man's downfall, he knew, but he'd like to try to trust this one.

"If I tell you, will you promise to keep it to yourself."

She picked up a dish towel and wiped her hands. "Of course. Wait. Should I be worried about this?"

"No. No. You'll understand in a minute."

"Okay." Her lips formed a straight line, as if she feared the worst kind of news.

"Do you know where Harney County is?"

"Yes, it's in the Owyhee Desert. South of here in Oregon, Southwest Idaho and North Nevada," she answered.

He nodded. "Well, the story goes that sometime during the 1870s, soldiers at Fort Harney were called to fight during an Indian uprising. They camped out in the desert and apparently one soldier found some gold nuggets. There was rumor of a mine in the area, but the soldiers were called to duty and couldn't search for it. When they had time to go back and search, no one found the hidden mine."

"That's an interesting tale, but what does that have to do with the here and now."

"My grandfather, Pops, said that his grandfather was a soldier who went back and found gold. He hid it somewhere and when he could make it back, brought it up here and buried it."

"Here? *Here?*" she asked with furrowed brow.

"Pops was the first generation to get close when we found this spot. He spotted the symbol of the sun way down on the rock. We planted a bush above it."

"But you've dug down so deep. Shouldn't you have found it by now?"

He rubbed his face with both hands. "I know it sounds strange but there is something to this."

"Okay. I'm listening," she said, probably not to frustrate him any further.

"Not everyone could read back then, so they left symbols and signs to direct them back to the treasure."

Faith pursed her lips, not a good sign, so he continued, "The etching of the sun, at the top of the hole I've dug, means opening."

He smiled to show his excitement, but she didn't return it. "To Murrayville?"

"It wasn't called Murrayville back then, you know," he

said with a chuckle. "Most of this was all wilderness, but people started to make it out here because of the gold rush."

Now her eyebrows nearly covered the tops of her eyes. Probably time to leave before she called him crazy, or something similar.

He slapped his thighs. "Well, enough story time. I think I better get going. Have things to do."

Her eyebrows were in the right place now, so she was probably glad he was on his way out.

"Thanks for the perfect lunch."

She'd turned back to the sink. "Welcome."

How stupid could he be? He wasn't thinking, that's what. He knew she never thought too much of him, blasting her window and all, but the way she just looked at him spoke volumes. She thought he was crazy.

Faith didn't particularly think he was on the right path in his career as well. He had lots of thoughts when it came to trial work, but he'd always asked for guidance and help to get him where he was today: Wanted by the best.

On the way back to the trailer, he stopped and stared down at the pit he'd carved into the ground. He could have told her he'd seen a snake with its head pointing down and a four-pointed star that meant danger. Humph.

Danger. That's for sure, and she lives right next door. Well, he wasn't out too much, just a little pride. And he did have a nice lunch.

Yet, he couldn't wave off the electricity he felt standing next to Faith.

He looked back toward her house and sighed. Suddenly tired, he moved away from the diggings and decided he'd spend a little time going over the notes he'd taken about the two firms that were interested in him. He couldn't keep knocking ideals back and forth in his head forever.

~

FAITH TOOK a dishcloth and wiped the table while she wondered just what she'd been thinking. She asked for this, she invited him over for a meal. A step closer to Brien and she would've been kissing a crazy man.

Harney County gold. She'd never heard of it. Sure, she knew there was gold around here, but this? Really?

CHAPTER 8

The moment Faith always knew would come was at hand. Her father, Casey Chadwick made it home in time for dinner. The tall man filled the door frame and a brunette woman stood behind him. She looked around the room timidly as Casey hugged his only child.

Faith believed she'd be fair and objective when her father decided to bring a woman home to meet her, but instead she felt suspicious.

"Gwen Ryan, meet my daughter and mayor of Murrayville, Faith Chadwick."

Gwen shook her hand and then put a hand on her chest. "I'm so glad to meet you. I've heard so much about you."

She wondered what her dad had told her. "Nice to meet you, too."

It had been eleven years since her mother died. The four-teen-year-old she'd been stirred inside, bringing the wound caused by such great loss to the surface. Memories flooded her mind.

*After basketball practice, Faith, starving, stopped by a fast food joint with two friends. They gobbled their food, laughing between bites about petty things. This day marked the end of her childhood as she knew it as her father met her at the front door of their home in tears. Tears she'd not seen on her father's face before or since. Casey could hardly say the words he had to say, and that was that her mother had died, her car smashed by a semi-truck on the highway.*

Faith hung onto this memory as she stood looking in the freezer. Finally, she shook her head and pulled out some hamburger patties to throw on the grill.

While her father showed Gwen the house, she set the patties in the microwave for a brief thaw, and then cut up the needed condiments.

She watched Gwen through the window as her father pointed here and there about the yard and beyond.

It was hard, like a stab to the heart, to see him with someone else besides her mother. Yet, she loved her father and wanted the best for him, as her mother would. She reminded herself that to love and be loved again was a good thing for him.

Faith knew she would always cherish their time alone together, just the two of them as a family, nevertheless, this is a new time and era for them both and they should carry on with their lives.

Her thoughts shifted to Brien as she caught a glimpse of his shirt sleeve in the brush. She only saw it because she knew he was there.

BRIEN SAT on a boulder and watched the sunshine through the forest, highlighting deciduous leaves blowing in the breeze. Yes, this was a great thinking place, and he had much to ponder.

He'd believed he had a gift, or calling, to be a lawyer, ever since debate honors in high school. Yet, when he applied for a job with the Walter, Simon, and Stimpson law firm he couldn't help but notice the elaborate offices, expensive suits and shoes on everyone from lawyers to clients. Even if he hadn't noticed, they pointed these things out to him. Walter also said he'd be making a six-figure salary at their firm upon accepting their offer, however, he'd have no choice on what client or clients he represented.

Brien went in again to talk to Simon, and he learned about a client wanting to sue a fellow socialite for defamation of character.

In these woods now, it all seemed so small. Did he want to serve the spoiled community that could afford his services, or did he want to help people who really needed him? Was it more important to serve for money or for fulfillment of soul?

He had so many more thoughts about what he deemed acceptable. He knew as a lawyer he was in the perfect position to act as a mediator. He could think of lawyers as adversaries that look out for each other, no one getting hurt, where everyone wins to some degree.

Voices came from Faith's backyard. He turned to see a man and a woman in the garden.

GWEN HELPED SET the table and Faith's dad pulled a kitchen chair out of the way and sat down.

"We're on our way to Nebraska; we'll leave tomorrow."

Faith shut the cupboard doors, and then spun around. "So soon?"

"Yes." He smiled at Gwen who returned it as if they had a little secret between them. "I'd like to take Gwen there and have her look around the town. If she likes what she sees, she'll apply for a teaching job there. Need a little time for that, and to get settled before school starts."

Faith turned back around and grabbed the cut-up condiments from the refrigerator, and Gwen took them from her and set them on the table.

As Faith reached back into the refrigerator for the mustard, a lump formed in her throat. Dad was leaving so soon; she had to share him now.

Gwen said, "I'm sorry we can't stay longer. I'd like to get to know you better, Faith."

Faith put on her best smile, said, "We have time in the future to get acquainted."

"I'm glad to hear that," said Gwen.

"Me, too," said her father as they sat down to eat.

Afterwards her father cleared the dishes and Gwen insisted she rinse them and put them in the dishwasher. Faith succumbed and sat next to her dad.

He put a hand to the back of her neck and rubbed it briefly as he'd done so many times before. The lump in her throat rose to the surface again.

"How's the town mayor?"

She focused on his words and the lump subsided. "Pretty good. Things are not too bad right now," she said with a half-smile.

He nodded. "Knew you'd be a good mayor. You have more good sense than I do."

"You were a good mayor, Dad."

"You were a mayor, Casey?" Gwen's eyes shown like a smitten teenager.

"Thought I told you. Guess not. Yes, did a couple of sentences, I mean two terms here."

"How impressive. And good for you, Faith, for stepping up to the job."

"She stepped up automatically, since she'd planned on it since she was ten years old."

"I'm still impressed. With both of you."

"When it's your town, you want it to be the best it can be," Faith added. "Thanks for cleaning up."

"My pleasure. How about a walk, Casey?"

"Sure. Want to come along, Faith?"

"No. You two go ahead. I'd like to weed a bit in the garden. It's such a nice evening."

Faith bent over to check on the tomato plants but didn't really see them. The whole situation with her father and Gwen shook her to her core.

Gwen seemed perfectly fine, and she hadn't seen her father act smitten with anyone since her mom died.

She took in a breath and then completely exhaled it all with an emotion that totally overcame her so that she dropped to her knees and sobbed. Even though she knew it was childish, she didn't want her father to replace her mother with someone else.

"Faith?"

Faith gasped and turned quickly fearing her father might catch her crying. She hadn't noticed a soul around her and was embarrassed to be found this way.

"Oh. Brien."

He'd heard the soul wrenching sobs. When he found out it wasn't an animal in distress, but a human, it was one of the saddest things he'd ever heard. He couldn't stop himself from going over to see if he could help in some way.

Faith stood up and tried to wipe her tears with the sleeve of her shirt.

"The onions get me every time."

"They're several feet from you, so I imagine they must be pretty strong."

She returned his smile. Kind of.

"I see you have company tonight."

"Yes. My father...and his girlfriend," she said between sobs.

"Oh, so that's your father." He didn't want her to cry again. Not knowing what to do, he stuck his hands in his pockets and looked out toward the mountains.

"I'm sorry," he said.

She smiled. "Thank you." After looking at her dirty hands, she wiped her tears with the other sleeve this time.

"I'm sorry his girlfriend doesn't meet your expectations."

"She does. I suppose that's the problem. I didn't know about her and I was caught off balance. The way my dad looks at her makes me know that our family is changing again. I really miss my mother right now. She died when I was fourteen."

"I'm sorry about your loss. I can't imagine life without my mother."

"Thanks, that helps." After looking at him for a moment, she reached down and plucked a cherry tomato, more orange than red, and stuck it in her mouth. "Want one?"

"Sure."

It tugged at his heart strings to see her like this. He wanted to do something to show he cared, so he took her hand, wanting to show his friendship and led her to the hole.

"I want to show you something. Let me help you down here."

*Oh, dear, what had she gotten herself into?* It had been all good, very caring of the man to gently take her hand in his. But she wasn't expecting this crazy stuff. Faith guessed she had time to humor him, not to mention a moment's reprieve from the grief she felt.

"Right here. I believe I told you this was the sun."

She nodded.

"It means opening. See this marking?"

"Yes."

"It's a slope with a little circle under it. It means slope, go down the hill. That is why I dug in this direction."

He put her hand along the line and the dot under it.

"This could be just a line with a circle under it, you know," she said.

Brien's lips went straight. "Of course, but there's more. After I blasted, I found this." He pointed to what looked like a four-cornered star. She couldn't fathom what this symbol meant.

"I have a chart in the trailer. I'll get it in a minute."

Good, she needed proof that he wasn't totally crazy. *Sun, stars, aliens...oh, my.*

"Anyway, this symbol is a four-pointed star meaning grave danger."

"Okay."

"Like I said before, the story goes that once you found gold, or some sort of valuables, you could be followed and robbed, so that's the reason the gold was buried. Many couldn't read or write, so they had to mark the spot some-way, so that they could come back later or send someone for it."

She nodded.

"The etchings are almost illegible as you can see."

"Yes," answered Faith. He had an energy about him that made his voice rise in excitement. Truly he believed what he said.

"So, you say there's actually a chart that explains these symbols?"

"Yes. While we're down here let me show you a couple more signs first."

Faith nodded. She was starting to come around, he could tell.

Brien hadn't planned on doing this, but her tears threw

him. He wanted her to come back to her strong, capable self, the one he knew could handle Murrayville. He wanted more than that, he wanted her to smile again, and this was the only thing he had in his possession at the time.

"This, right over here, is a spade shaped like a triangle at the end, which means dig here."

She took an intake of breath and smiled. "I see that."

*That's my girl.* "Right over here is a cross, but the cross has many meanings, so your guess is as good as mine."

They crawled out of the hole and brushed their hands off on their pants in unison.

Brien stepped into the trailer, then back out with a paper in his hand.

"Oh, my goodness," she said when she noticed near replicas. "Oh, my goodness."

He didn't seem so crazy after all. Still it was hard to believe that he could find something after all these years.

"Faith!" she heard her father call.

She turned to call back at him, but Brien put a hand on her arm.

"I'd rather keep this secret if you don't mind. How about I don't tell him you were crying, and you don't tell him about buried gold?"

Her eyes widened in apparent shock for a moment and then narrowed. "I suppose that's fair."

"Do you want me to stay out of sight?"

"It's up to you. I will tell him that we do have a neighbor out here."

He nodded. "Maybe I'll wait until another time to come out and meet him."

MAYOR FAITH CHADWICK tried so hard to keep her professional image up. Brien realized that now, after seeing her so vulnerable. As a matter of fact, she was so human it made him take far more than a second look at her. Her tears stirred him greatly; he was at her side in a millisecond, wanting to do something to help her. What he'd done was give away the path to the gold, that is, if it was still here. A woman *was* his downfall, apparently.

Whether there was buried gold, and anything to worry about, he didn't know. It all seemed surreal to him; however, the clues were fascinating and kept him going. It's just that he felt so alone with his grandfather gone, and probably why he reached out to Faith.

FAITH WOULDN'T TELL anyone about what Brien was doing. *She* wasn't crazy. She didn't want to bring intruders out here, with speculations about why a handsome, available man was practically in her backyard.

Faith could hear the tongues wagging now. Not to mention the hordes of men coming to claim the so-called gold themselves. *Humph.*

She wondered why he'd even told her. He'd seemed so protective of what he was doing until now. Why was that? She thought back to recent interactions and she couldn't think of a reason to tell her. It seems he told her about the treasure to amuse her, to dry her tears. But why would he do that? Why would he care? Yet, she didn't like that he'd black-mailed her to make sure she didn't say anything.

"SOMEONE SEEMS to be camping next door. Do you know anything about that, Faith?"

"Yes. Uh…he's doing some mining, has a legal claim to do so."

Casey's eyes narrowed. "I wonder why he picked a claim so close to the house."

"He had mined here before our house was built. With his grandfather."

"He's not a seedy sort, is he?" asked Gwen.

Faith took in a breath of air. "No, he's a lawyer; recently passed the bar."

"I'd think he'd do better mining for gold around Murray Creek," said her father.

"Yeah, I told him that. I'm thinking he has a sentimental reason for being right here. His grandfather passed away recently." Well, she did think that, but that was hardly the whole of it.

"I know how that goes," Casey said, and looked at Gwen after she put her hand on his shoulder in an empathetic way.

He looked back at Faith. "Do you feel safe out here alone with him nearby?"

"Yes. I don't think his plans have anything to do with me."

"He's married then?" asked her father.

"Thanks for your vote of confidence, but his world really doesn't revolve around me. He's only here for a time and then he goes to work at some big firm."

"What does he look like?" Gwen asked.

"He's handsome, if that's what you mean."

Gwen's eyes widened.

"What?" Faith answered a little too irritated. "Even if this man was interested in me, the mayor is not after a scandal, so please, Dad, keep this quiet."

He moved over to the window. "Okay. I guess."

"Thanks, I appreciate it."

And just like that they were gone, leaving her alone and bereft.

Faith shook her head. Of course, she was single and on her own, just as she'd been yesterday. She wasn't an orphan, she told herself. She'd no doubt have a stepmother soon, to treat like a friend if nothing else and she could do that.

The sun was about to set when she heard a noise on the front porch. *Perhaps it's just one of the feral cats from around here*, but the idea didn't make her feel any safer.

She'd just finished fixing herself a glass of lemonade, so she set it on the counter and dried her hands with a dishcloth.

The front door creaked as it opened, slowly, and she was certain the hair on the back of her neck stood up. Roger let out a low growl. Without thinking, she ran out the back door and through the woods to Brien's, Roger at her heels. She used her fist to knock on his trailer door.

"Whoa! What's wrong?" He came out the door and she moved behind him; her front tucked neatly behind his back.

"Someone's trying to get in my house."

"What?" he asked then looked toward the house.

She peeked around him and searched the area as well. No one was in sight.

"Let's go check it out," he said.

"No, not yet. I really got spooked. Can I stay here a few minutes with you?"

"We'll just check it out, Faith."

"Oh," she said in a small apprehensive voice.

He took a deep breath and stepped back into his trailer. When he came back out, he carried a backpack with one hand. After a couple of steps, Faith moved behind him three paces. Roger rushed ahead.

Roger slipped around the side of the house. Brien moved to the back porch where he took the steps and opened the screen door. "Anybody home?"

Faith heard nothing.

"Anybody here?" he said, louder this time. No response, so he stepped inside.

Nothing was amiss in the kitchen, so they moved to the living room where the front door stood open.

"Anybody here?" he called out again.

Brien looked at her with raised eyebrows, as if in question. She didn't want to be left alone, so she moved behind him like a shadow when he checked every room, under beds, and in closets. He didn't see anything amiss, except for the open front door.

After shutting the door, Brien took her arm and moved her so that they were eye to eye. Her breathing slowed to match his and her eyes no longer moved from side to side in panic.

"You've been through a lot today, Faith."

She shook her head vigorously.

He took her hand. "You've found out your dad has a new love and it's taken an emotional toll on you."

She looked down and shook her head again.

"Then you thought someone came into your house, when you were already upset, and your brain played a trick on you."

"No. I heard a noise…uh, footsteps on the porch. The door opened."

"Your father left, and you were feeling alone and vulnerable."

She sniffed and her chin wobbled. "That may be true, but I did hear something, and Roger growled."

Faith turned, as if he'd hurt her feelings and he felt awful.

"Faith?"

"It's okay, I'll just say goodnight now."

Her feelings were on her sleeve, and she didn't need to have Brien around to see it. She was the town mayor, for goodness sake.

He didn't believe her anyway, believed her to be a nut case, which was disconcerting to say the least.

Instead of leaving, Brien sat down on her couch and set his backpack at his feet. "I'll just stay here tonight. Make sure everything's okay."

Faith crossed her arms, then uncrossed them, not knowing what to do. She was emotionally drained and exhausted. And worst of all, needy.

## CHAPTER 9

*O*ne word that described Faith was tough. A woman not afraid to state her opinion and speak the truth when it came to representing her town. Now, she'd lost her way, disturbed by her past and now her future.

Brien watched her, waiting for her to say something, but she didn't seem to have the power to do so. She needed help but couldn't request or deny it now.

"I'd feel better if you weren't alone. I'll just sleep on your couch. Do you have a pillow I can use?"

She nodded and went to the linen closet.

"Here. And thanks."

"No problem. Really. I think I hear Roger on the porch. I'll let him in."

After he let Roger in and locked the door, Faith stepped in front of Brien and thought about how needy she was. This was not the type of woman she wanted to be. She needed to buck up somehow, and she would.

Brien looked back at her, no doubt waiting for her to say something. Instead she turned and took the stairs to her bedroom to try and gather herself, so that she could go to sleep with a possible intruder on the loose and a hunk of a man in her house.

MARTY HAD BEEN at the door and if it wasn't for the stupid mongrel frightening Faith, he'd be spending time with her right now. He quickly exited the house and stood back in the trees and watched Faith run into the woods in the opposite direction. On closer examination, he saw that she'd run to a trailer next door, the mutt beside her. A light from the window confirmed someone was living in the trailer, which he did not know.

He took a moment to watch for movement in the trailer, and when he didn't see anything, he moved closer to the window.

Faith was worried all right, and he didn't mean for her to feel this way. If anything, he wanted to help her spend a cozy evening at home, getting to know him better. He'd planned it so that she'd come to understand that he was her soulmate.

Now, she was leaving the trailer and a man with a back-pack was following her. To keep from attracting the mutt he took off the other way back to his truck. Fortunately, the dog didn't chase after him, only went a little way beyond the house and then apparently circled back.

His anger drove his steps harder and faster back through the woods. He didn't expect or want a man near Faith. This would not do, at all.

He believed that when you had a problem with your girl-friend, then you need to approach *her* with it, not her boyfriend.

Boyfriend, he thought bitterly and wanted to roar. He had to stop these two before she was completely lost to her real mission in life, to be his lover and wife. But, for now, she had to be punished. A sinner needed to be disciplined, so that they could walk the straight and narrow path again. It was as simple as that.

~

FAITH SPENT the next two days putting together class materials and then preparing the agenda for a council meeting.

Even though the Murrayville mayor was the highest ranking official, it didn't give her much power. She oversees the public service departments and was responsible for the safety of the town's people. She also had the power to sign permits and close public buildings deemed unsafe or due to riot situations. Besides that, she was the leader of the council meeting, represented the people, could put together new laws, but only had one vote, same as the other council members.

She could veto the council's proposal if she deemed it necessary, yet the council could override her decision. Aww, it was a fine line and she was grateful that no one had asked her to define just how this worked.

It was not a glamorous position, she often reminded herself, especially when you had to hire and direct professional services. Or, submit to low wages. Fortunately, she didn't have to work full-time as well.

Members of the community signed up to speak their mind for three minutes and then council members assembled in and took their seats.

Faith so wanted each meeting to go on in a professional manner but there was always a couple of people that worried her, people far left and far right in their thinking. Most of the time they were respectful of each other, but the going back and forth with opinions could be grueling. Today, Faith wouldn't have to use her mayor authority to close the building due to rioting and that was a good day in her book.

After the explanation of the budget, Faith called out the first name on the list of concerned public members. "Please introduce yourself to everyone here."

"My name is Marty Walker. I work at the public library here in town."

Faith thought he looked familiar but apparently couldn't place him out of the library. "Yes. Continue," she said with a smile.

Marty felt joy bubble up in his chest because of the special smile she gave him. "Thank you, mayor. I've been wanting to make mention of the state of the library building. Besides painting here and there over the years, it has had very little updating. Especially as compared to some of the other buildings in town." After a thorough explanation, he added, "I have some thoughts I'd like to share with you later, Ms. Chadwick, if you don't mind."

"I've been running some things through my mind lately about Main Street, but I'm not done with my research. Come back to the next meeting and I will have some answers to share, one way or the other."

Marty didn't really care about the condition of the library but was only here for Faith. He was irritated that she didn't offer to stay and speak with him, but she asked him back to the next council meeting. That was something. She wants him back; he can help her. Yes, he could *help* her. "I will look forward to coming back to the next meeting, then."

Yet, he was pretty sure, he'd see her before then.

Faith thought it strange that someone would express an element of passion about looking forward to an upcoming council meeting. Also, he didn't look at any council members, only herself, like they had some sort of connection. Suddenly she remembered the conversation she had with her friend Rose Langley at her office, saying he was single, a widower.

No, she didn't want it to be attraction. Even if her thoughts weren't on Brien most of the day, she didn't feel any kind of attraction to Marty, no matter how interested he was in the community.

JUST BEFORE THE sun went down, Brien built a fire in a covered aluminum fire pit that he'd bought in town. He thought about all the digging and sweeping he'd done by hand and now felt the effects of the workout.

As the darkness progressed so did the number of lights in Faith's house. He scooted his chair over enough to see if he could spot her. Movement caught his eye, so he stood and moved closer, standing mostly behind a pine tree.

There she was moving about, her ponytail swinging behind her. Suddenly he longed for company. Not just any company, hers.

He wondered if he had the chance to meet her at another place and time whether they'd hook up. A point when she wasn't concerned with her image in town, and he wasn't so worried about secretly finding gold.

Her hands went up over her head and lingered in a stretch. She seemed to be as tired as he was. When she started to turn off lights for the night, he turned back to the fire. Something in the distance, a small globe of light, caught in his peripheral vision but when he turned it was gone. Perhaps his tired eyes had played tricks on him. No one would be out here walking around this time of night.

MOVEMENT CAUGHT FAITH'S EYE. Brien was walking to the front of the house. She met him at the front door.

"Good morning, Faith."

"Good morning. Come in."

"I can see you're getting ready to go to work, but I have a question to ask you."

"Sure. Sit down."

"I can stand."

He stood there a moment and then cleared his throat. "Would you be interested in going to Portland for supplies?"

"Shopping? I suppose I would be, depending on the day." She had a feeling that there was something more because he rubbed a hand through his hair then fidgeted with a few coins in his pocket. "What's the deal, McGrew?"

He sighed and they both sat down. "A prospective employer asked me to a dinner party. He wants me to bring a date."

"Me?"

He nodded.

Faith couldn't believe he'd be so shy about asking someone out, especially as a friend. She put a hand to her mouth to stifle a chuckle.

He frowned, then rubbed his chin.

She massaged her forehead with her thumb and fore-finger and concentrated on being serious. "Don't you know anyone closer to Portland that you don't have to take shopping as well?"

"Yes, I do, but you're the first woman I thought of, because-"

When he stopped talking, she crossed her arms and waited for words such as beautiful or sexy. Or, perhaps he wanted an exquisite trophy girlfriend at his side. She uncrossed her arms, stood straighter and smiled in antic-ipation.

"I wanted to take a woman of substance."

"A woman of substance?" She supposed that's what she got for thinking so highly of her looks.

He didn't answer her, just gave her direct eye contact, which ended up making her turn away. Could he be pleading with her? she wondered.

"I see it means a lot to you."

"Yes," he said and nodded quickly, twice.

This behavior seemed so foreign to anything she'd learned about him so far. To be honest, it raised her curiosity up several notches. She wanted to ask more questions. In time, she thought, in time.

"Okay."

He let out a burst of air and smiled.

"Will the dress be casual?"

He shook his head. "You'll need to bring a dress. Do you have anything nice?"

"I have a dress that will work."

When he left, she reached for her work bag and turned toward the window instead of the door. He wanted her because he needed a woman of substance. What better person to bring than a mayor when searching for a job? Don't be thinking anything else, she told herself.

$\mathcal{B}$rien watched Faith lock her door and move toward him with an overnight bag, a red dress on a hanger and a paper in hand.

"Top of the morning," Brien called out.

"Top of the morning to you too, McGrew."

Good, she was in a good mood.

"I've made a supply list," she said. "It doesn't matter to me if we shop sometime today or in the morning. Suit yourself."

"I thank you for the options. I brought a cooler, so we have choices. We'll see how we feel when we get to the big city."

"Good. I'm ready to leave town."

"Oh?"

Through narrowed eyes, she said, "No, nothing's wrong. I've just spent time putting together and then submitting information for a grant. It's just nice to have a break from all things normal, and of course do a little shopping."

"And a nice dinner."

She smiled. "Yes, and a nice dinner."

Because of ample rainfall each year, Portland became a

green and beautiful place. She'd always enjoyed Portland this time of year when flowers were still in bloom and fewer gray days.

Brien drove into a Portland motel parking lot and upon registering inside, Faith noted he asked for two separate rooms without an adjoining door. She let out a slow breath of relief.

BRIEN HAD THOUGHT he'd seen Faith at her finest, whether in a business suit and high heels, to a casual, natural beauty that few could pull off. Yet, at this moment he was speechless.

"Let me just grab my handbag," she said with her hand on the handle of the motel room's door.

He nodded. She wore a sleek, red sleeveless dress with matching high heel sandals that buckled at the ankle. When she turned, he could see that the back side of the dress sported a low-cut apex. It was as if her back played a game of hide and seek with her hair.

"You look nice," he said.

"You don't look so bad yourself."

He smiled. "This old thing? Thanks."

"Old? I don't think so. I'm tempted to look at the label."

"No touching until after dinner," he said,

with index finger up.

"Keep hoping."

AFTER DRIVING ACROSS PORTLAND, they came upon the city of Lake Oswego. It was a high-class place to live, so Faith wasn't surprised to learn they'd headed that way.

Brien pulled into a paved driveway that bypassed the

house. They parked with other cars at the edge of the yard. From her vantage point, she could see the lake. She turned to gaze at the vast house, a Colonial three-story brick structure with white columns across the front.

"I feel a little out of place here, Brien."

"You do? Aren't there a couple of big shots in Murrayville?"

"Sure, we have a retired Senator and the owner of one of the largest ranches in the state, but that's it. I'm afraid this group will be a little out of my element."

"Relax."

"You're not a little nervous meeting with someone who may hold your future in his or her hands?" she asked.

"Not with you on my arm."

"Oh, *come on.*"

"Maybe some nervousness, but I'm here mostly to watch, take it all in. I've worked hard to get here, and I take it very seriously."

"What will you be watching?" she asked, this time with a

serious tone, wanting him to feel calm and assured before entering.

"That I don't know yet."

"Fair enough answer."

"Mr. Stimpson, this is Faith Chadwick."

Calvin Stimpson pumped her hand. "It's nice to meet a friend of Brien's."

"The pleasure is mine, Mr. Stimpson, and this must be your wife."

Calvin's eyes rounded as though he'd forgotten she was there. Mrs. Stimpson's lips formed a straight line when her husband looked her way. She put an empty glass on a passing tray and took another drink.

"Mrs. Stimpson," said Faith and shook her free hand.

The smile she returned to Faith didn't look real. She also received a visual once over.

"I don't think I've seen you around."

"No, you haven't. I live in Murrayville."

"Where?" she asked, her eyes moving from Faith to Calvin.

"It's a small town in Northeast Oregon," said Faith.

"I don't think I know where that is."

"Faith is the mayor of Murrayville," said Brien in an upbeat tone.

"Well, is that right?" Mr. Stimpson gave her a pat on the shoulder. "That's a lot to accomplish at your age. You've got spunk and determination, I like that."

"Well, my father-"

"Yes. She does have that," Brien shot in, cutting her off.

Calvin took her arm as a symbol they were moving to another area. Mrs. Stimpson turned away without any explanation, but two other men took her place. The five of them entered a room through what looked like partially hand carved wooden doors into a library of such she'd never seen. Rows of built-in bookcases surrounded the room and a huge desk sat in the center with two wing-backed chairs in front. A marble fireplace, with two stuffed chairs in front, stood at one end.

"How about bourbon all the way around, Bobby?" asked Calvin.

"Yes, of course." Bobby went over to a short bar and started pouring the drinks. Brien took one. Faith hated bourbon and wanted to decline but took one anyway. She could take a sip and instead of drinking more, hold the goblet all evening if she had to.

The men talked about their current case. She thought that Brien asked smart questions, but then what did she know about the business? All she knew was that he had dreams, either to become rich working with these people or do something on his own to help society.

As the evening progressed, and they'd joined the other patrons, piano music came through an elaborate speaker system. A few of the attendees danced to a slow tune and she set her glass of Bourbon on an end table and took Brien's hand.

"What, you want to dance?" he asked her.

She was determined to have some fun away from Murrayville, and it hadn't even started to happen.

"Yes, I'm a sucker for a slow dance. Come on," she said.

"Okay but guard your feet."

Faith stopped pulling him closer and took a step back to give him some space. She watched as he slowly scanned the room as if looking for something or someone that wasn't there yet. After a time of this, she did pull him to her, and she gained his total focus.

"You're working too hard, Brien. Take a break."

"Yes ma'am. You smell good."

She smiled and said, "I was going to say the same thing to you."

"What do you think of these people, Faith," he asked in her ear.

"I don't know. While you focused on the lawyers, I walked around. I can usually move through a room, listen to people talk and find someone I'd like for a friend. Yet, out of these people, I haven't come up with one that I could strike up a conversation with and enjoy. I mean no offense to you, Brien."

"I think I know what you're saying. I have more in common with the people in this room, because I know the business. Maybe I should say, I'm still learning the business."

"Calvin looks your way a lot, which makes me think that he really wants you on his team."

"Oh really? I thought he was looking at you," he said and smiled.

"Maybe a couple of the drunk guys are looking at me," she replied.

"Yes, people are starting to slur their words, so we can get going," he added.

He took her hand and they moved toward Calvin to shake his hand and say good-bye.

"I want you to join us, Brien." Brien didn't answer right away, and Calvin frowned before saying, "Now don't make me beg."

"I won't sir. I will give you an answer by the end of this next week."

"I'll think positive thoughts then," he said, smiling now.

As they walked through the front door, Faith said, "Can you make a decision by that time?"

"I don't know, but the way he looked at me there for a second, I had better."

Brien opened the passenger door of his truck for her, and she slid onto the seat. She noticed Brien had a frown on his face as he walked around the front of the truck and opened the door.

Before starting the car, he said, "Shouldn't every new attorney want this high paying, status building job?"

It sounded to her like he was asking her opinion, and that was almost sad, because she had no experience in this field. "I'd say many would want this job. I'd say some would want something else. You are the only one that knows how you truly feel. It seems you have conflicting beliefs inside, and one will win out, whether it's in one week or in years to come."

"You're not making this easy for me," he said, but smiled.

"Apparently, it's not at all easy for you. It'll come, it'll come."

"Does it impress you at all that I have a couple of good offers?"

"It doesn't have anything to do with me." After a moment, she added, "Okay, I suppose I'm impressed with your high grades and work ethic the most."

They were silent on the way to the motel, and Faith knew somehow that he needed the silence. She couldn't help but notice he wasn't overjoyed by this job offer.

He parked the truck, took a deep breath and looked her in the eye. "I'll walk you to your room."

"Well, thank you, sir."

"Let me open the door for you." He took the key card, swiped it and opened the door. She walked under his arm into the room.

"You still smell good," he said.

"Nothing makes a girl feel better than to hear she smells good," she replied.

"Well, you said I smell good."

"Yes, I did. Come here and kiss me goodnight," she said with a wide smile.

"Okay, if I have to."

Between the microwave and a round wooden table they stood, looking into each other's eyes. They came together awkwardly, and then stepped back. Faith could tell he was as confused as she was, whether to come back together or not.

She supposed this was a natural occurrence as they were two healthy adults. He smiled, barely, then a full smile and a dimple formed on his cheek. No doubt, he knew he had a charming smile and he used it just now. So, what was he doing, encouraging her?

Something stirred inside her as their eyes held and abruptly Brien lost his smile. The longer their eyes connected, the deeper the stirring.

"What was that?" she asked, just above a whisper.

"It felt good whatever it was."

Curiosity hit her again and she stepped closer.

He put both hands on her shoulders as if to keep her from moving closer, or was it to keep her from shifting away? They stood in this position; eyes connected until she had to look away. He was on his way to melting her into a puddle on the floor.

"I'm sorry," he said. "I don't know about us. I can't have the people of Murrayville know any more about me, that I'm looking for gold."

Her eyes had been something close to enchanted as she looked at him, shining and smiling. Now, they seemed cold and hard, not what he wanted at all.

Faith stood straight as a pole, arms to her sides. "I'm the one who should be sorry, I asked for a kiss. Goodnight, Brien. Sleep well."

In the doorjamb, he turned to say, "I didn't mean that the way it came out-"

Thankfully, he stepped back, because the door closed in his face.

He was right, she knew. Faith only wished she'd said it first. If he was embarrassed of her, he wouldn't have taken her to meet a perspective employer. So, she had to calm down, and be grateful that this, whatever it was, didn't go any farther. She had as much of a reason to keep him hid, down in the hole, looking for treasure.

Faith was nearly mortified for throwing herself at him. She was not that kind of girl, but he'd made her start to doubt her solid beliefs in a record amount of time. That kind of relationship was not to her liking anyway.

Now in his room, Brien stepped back from the door and wondered what in the world had happened. He'd always ruled with his head, but he barely escaped this time. Yet, he didn't want her mad at him, he couldn't bear the idea of it.

He sat down on his bed and thought about Faith. She was the first woman he'd come across that he wanted to share his feelings with, wanted to know what she thought of his job offers.

After shaking his head several times, he concluded that she was merely a woman that he was impressed with. A smart woman, who'd been around more blocks than he had in his life so far. He wanted a smart girl of her caliber to help him figure out what to do, that was the only reason he asked for her opinion.

The sad thing was, since his grandfather died, he couldn't figure out anything for himself. He'd gone through the motions of getting a mining claim and digging for gold, because that was always what they had planned to do. That was it, he couldn't move on.

Now, for some reason he wanted to latch on to Faith, and he didn't really know exactly why. Besides her being smart, beautiful and kind, she was basically amazing. Yet, what male wouldn't notice her, want to spend time with her?

After letting out a groan, he fell back in the bed and stared at the ceiling. He couldn't even make the decision to be her friend. He was pitiful by anyone's standard.

# CHAPTER 11

*A*fter little sleep, Faith showered and dressed in jeans and a t-shirt before going to get the continental breakfast.

Just off the office, Brien nodded at her from the toaster, where he buttered an English muffin. Instead of smiling, she nodded back. She certainly hoped breakfast would give her the boost her emotions needed and reached for as many high protein foods as her plate would hold.

It would be weird not to sit by Brien, she decided, and moved toward his table. She didn't like that she still harbored some negativity toward him and anticipated the bad vibes going away as they shopped and drove back to Murrayville together.

When the big box store opened, they waddled in with others looking for a good deal. She pulled her list from her purse and focused on what she needed.

In between the produce and the bakery, Brien said, "I know that I want us to be friends, Faith."

"Don't you have a list?" she shot back.

"No, not really. I only need a few things."

"Well, the perishables are right there," she said, and used her thumb to point behind her.

"Okay, I get it. We'll talk in the truck."

They did have to talk sooner later, she knew. What was wrong with her? Why did he affect her so? she wondered as she picked up paper towels. Then later, when she grabbed a box of yogurt. And even later when she found vitamins and pistachios. Finally, at the checkout counter, she concluded that having a lawyer as a friend might be a good thing one day. She'd focus on that.

They loaded up the back of Brien's truck with their purchases and he pulled a tarp out and over the contents, then tied it down firmly.

In the cab of the truck, he decided he could probably hear a pin drop. Finally, he said, "Haven't you ever been rejected, Faith?"

"What made you say that?" she asked and crossed her arms.

"You are still mad at me."

"Let's talk about something else."

"Okay," he said. "Do you plan to stay in Murrayville after your term is up?"

"You mean my term as mayor?"

"Yes."

"Yes. I like visiting a large town, but don't think I want to live there."

"How about you? Big town, little town?" she asked.

"I know that larger towns have more clientele for an attorney. That's all I know for sure. It must be nice to know what you want before hitting thirty."

"I want to work to make Murrayville a better place to live. That I know. We lose so many of our young people after high school or college to larger cities. That's hard on the people of Murrayville."

"Do you have a way to change this? *Is* there a way to change this?" he asked.

"That's a good question and one I haven't been able to get my head around. I just applied for a grant to help improve the store fronts of our Main Street businesses. I think we should keep the historical look but restore or freshen it up. Make it a town that people want to visit, a place for people to walk through the stores and purchase items that add to the economy."

"Maybe Murrayville needs to put in a big box store. Have more jobs that way. The youth of town just might stay."

"But the big box stores will take main street business away."

"Sounds like we have opposite views, doesn't it?" he asked.

"I don't know if I'd say that. All views should be considered. I've always believed that, but then I've thought about politics for a long time, Brien. We don't really have a middle class in Murrayville, just lower and upper. We also have a lot of retirees coming in from different places, those that don't need a job to live here."

"Huh."

"I must say I'm sorry for being mad at you, Brien. Yes, I've had a crush on you, probably since the first time I saw you. After the fear subsided, anyway."

He laughed out loud.

"Yes, I have been rejected, two major times, actually. Both during my time as a mayor. I'm on people's watch list and if I have a boyfriend, I become something like a celebrity. Truly, people of Murrayville are like the royal watchers. I couldn't have dinner out with my boyfriend without people talking about it like I wasn't even there. Both boyfriends felt like they couldn't make a move in town without everyone watching them and judging whether they were good enough for me."

"Are you sure about all that?" he asked with furrowed brow.

"You don't believe me?"

"No, I wouldn't say that. But just maybe they didn't want to settle down in Murrayville. Maybe it wasn't about you after all."

"Here I am trying to calm down and you're stirring me up again. I can only judge this by what they told me, Brien."

"They were jerks, Faith."

"That's what people have said, so maybe I should start believing it. Anyway, that is why I've been hiding since you've arrived. It's tough to have peering eyes watching me disgrace myself with another man. I don't want to go there again," she said firmly, staring at him with chin up.

"Don't worry, I'll try to keep my distance, if that's what you want, Faith."

"You already drew the line, back at the motel. And rightly so," she replied.

"That was about me, not about you. That was about my being alone to find the gold."

"Okay," she said. "Let's turn the tables. If you find the gold, what then? Will you still take one of the jobs in Portland?"

"That's a good question, Faith. Thanks for asking. I need to think of this with a different perspective."

"How sure are you that you will find it?" she asked, half turning toward him.

"I'm not sure at all. I only wish that Pops was with me. If he was, I think maybe I'd be able to figure out what I really want in life. Pops would not be persuaded by a bunch of rich lawyers; I can tell you that."

"Maybe that's something of an answer for you. But you

must live up to your conscience, not your grandfather's. Ethics and ideals don't have anything to do with feelings, Brien."

"And you should stop hiding, you are far too special of a woman to hide away because of what other people might think of you. I know that you are too strong for that. Don't let anything like that happen to you again," he said, his voice rising. "I mean it."

"Thanks. I like bantering with you, Brien."

"Back at ya."

FAITH WALKED to her mailbox and pulled out the correspondences. One came from the foundation in which she'd applied for the storefront grant. Her heart pounded in her chest and her legs grew weak. She had counted on this grant so much, far too much for something that seemed as likely as winning the lottery. Still, she had to know, good or bad, she couldn't just stare at the envelope.

She set her purse down and used both hands to open the letter. She studied the first page of the document and her whole world steadied. Next, she put her things inside and let Roger out of the house.

Roger raced Faith to Brien, where she threw her arms around his neck.

"I got it! I got it!" She hopped up and down.

"You're going to get yourself dirty. I'm filthy."

"Oh, it doesn't matter," she said near his face. "I got the grant, Brien!"

Brien watched her eyes sparkle and flash in the sunlight, before tearing up. Never had he seen her so beautiful as at this moment and he felt some sort of twang inside his chest, making him realize that he wanted to be the reason for this delighted face. It stunned him that those emotions came so quickly to the surface.

"What's the matter, Brien? Are you not happy for me?"

"No, I am. I'm very happy for you and for Murrayville, of course."

"Oh, my goodness, I'm going to call a few council members, they will be so excited. I will talk to you later, Brien. Come on, Roger." She turned and jogged the best she could in heels, around protruding rocks, toward her house.

THE NEXT MORNING AT WORK, Faith cleared the manila file folders from the top of her desk. So excited about the changes coming to Murrayville, she wanted to get out and talk to the people. She decided to start at phase one, the library, the first to experience the structural changes.

Marty Walker looked up from his desk and gave Faith a big smile.

"Hi. You must have heard the good news," she said.

"No. I'm just glad to see you. What can I do for you? What's the news?"

"I submitted a grant to improve the store fronts and it was accepted. Phase one is to start at the library here. I knew you'd be pleased."

Marty was...to see her, he couldn't care less about the library storefront. His heart leaped thinking she was here to see him on a personal level, but no, she was excited about something else.

His gaze moved over her from head to toe and watched Faith's lips as she spoke. Her full lips stretched into a smile and he realized even more how beautiful she was. And he desperately wanted to touch her.

Up close and personal was what he wanted and figured

this might be the chance he'd be looking for to spend some quality time with her.

He listened to her explain the grant and the changes to happen to the front of the library.

After moving to the front of the building and looking at the old leaded windows, she turned and smiled again. He took her arm as they walked back to his desk.

"I suppose I should go and leave you to your work," she said at length.

"Oh, no. Don't do that."

She looked at him and then looked down, her smile lost now.

"I mean, I'd like to hear about every detail. I am loving this idea of making some changes to this old building."

She smiled then, and his heart sped up again. Her smile made him know without a doubt that she cared for him. He would enjoy working closely with her. Finally, this was the chance he'd really been waiting for.

"Well, I'm afraid I don't have enough information yet," she said. "I'll be sure to let you know the details when I do. Thanks for your time."

With that she wiggled off and he watched her every move to and out the door. Then from the front window as she walked to her car and until she was clear out of sight.

He couldn't remember ever being this stoked about a woman before. His heart told him, again, that she would be his. Things were coming together the way he'd hoped.

Something about Marty Walker made Faith feel uneasy. She couldn't put her finger on just what it was, but the feeling lurked around her like a dark cloud. A feeling she'd felt only a few times before, once in a haunted house and another time when she came across the murder of crows while jogging. Perhaps the old library was haunted, she thought. It made sense to her. If she was a spirit she'd want to hang around books in the hereafter. Faith smiled at the course her thoughts had taken her.

She shook her head and pulled her car away from the curb and headed back to her office.

Back at the office, Faith caught Rose Langley filing the files she's stacked before she left. "Aww, you're so sweet," Faith told her with a smile.

"Oh, hello," she returned. "You look happy." After taking in a breath, she said, "Oh, you've met someone. I knew it would only be a matter of time."

Rose put a file down and massaged around the gnarled knuckles of her right hand.

"Slow down, sister. I'm happy because my grant was accepted. We are going to have some nice store fronts here on our Main Street."

"Is that all?" she asked disappointed.

Faith chuckled. She guessed someone had to take over the role of mother in her life. "Aren't you happy for me? Proud of me?"

"Yes, I've always been proud of you and I doubt that will ever change. But anyone can paint a storefront, you know."

"Oh, you are too cute, Rose. Let me help you with that, so you don't have to be on your feet too long."

"Well, I keep hearing that exercise is good for you, so here I am."

"I'm glad you're here to exercise with me."

"You sure you haven't met someone?"

Well, she'd have to say she had, but nothing to talk to her about. Rose would be planning a wedding if she did. "I'll let you know when something lasting comes along."

As Faith finished filing with Rose, she thought about Brien. Not too surprising since he'd been on her mind for some time now. Before long he would be leaving for a job in Portland. She'd miss him when he was gone and probably look out her bedroom window and try to imagine him next door. That is very sad, she told herself and then tried to refocus on the grant.

Still, as she drove home, she slowed down in front of Brien's claim to see if she could spot him. She knew where to look, at the edge of the big pine tree where he'd usually hide when someone drove by. She knew because she'd hidden there with him, and the thought made her smile in reflection. He stepped out in the clearing when he saw her car, but she drove on to let Roger out so he could do his daily run around the woods.

Roger barked a hello, took a dog treat from her, and out the door he ran. To Brien. Oh well, she'd get the mail and then simply mosey over to see about her dog.

Faith set her mail on a chair, changed her shoes and went to Brien's. She found him sitting on a large rock, petting Roger. Roger's tail hit Brien's side repeatedly as he welcomed her.

"How's the town?" he asked.

"Oh, fair to middling," she said. "You know, one of these days you're going to dig so deep you won't be able to climb out and I haven't decided if I will help you out or not." She crossed her arms and smiled. "You about done, yet?"

He chuckled. "I can see what you mean. Even though I doubt my great-whatever-grandpa would've put the gold down this deep—"

"Yes," she cut in. "I thought about that myself. Especially if he was alone. I mean, how long did he have to bury the gold before someone came along? And for that matter, why didn't he come back to get it?"

He nodded. "Pops said not long after he left what we call the armed services today he got sick and when he didn't improve, his wife helped him draw a map using some sort of code before he died. By the time Pops got ahold of it, there wasn't much left to see due to wear and tear. Pops searched with his father as a boy, so he gained a few facts from him. My dad said he wasn't interested in following a myth, and it seemed to hurt Pops that he wouldn't go look with him."

"But you did, Brien."

"I did and I know now it's more about the search and the time with family. That's what's important. My dad missed more than he will ever know by not going with Pops."

She nodded. "You've been blessed to have been able to spend so much time with your grandfather. That's treasure in itself."

"I'm glad you understand." His eyes misted and he raised an arm to wipe an eye with the sleeve of his t-shirt. He cleared his throat. "There's a reason I'm digging so deep... besides being crazy. Pop told me about the Spaniards in the early 1500s, when they couldn't read as well as we do now. So, they made symbols to mark where they put their treasure, in case they had to flee the area. Sometimes they had to have a friend come back and get the treasure for them."

"What, the Spaniards came here? Murrayville?"

"Around here apparently. Pops said that a guy told him he'd seen some carvings, but he didn't say where exactly, only in the area. For that matter, even Native Americans hid treasure. Church treasure had been stolen and buried as well."

Faith frowned and squinted at him. "But why so deep?"

Brien stood. "Okay." He rubbed his hands together. "According to what I read, Spain took the average height of a man in the 1500s and it's about five-feet-seven inches. Spain then stated that the depth of the treasure was to be buried at least five-foot-seven inches down. Some say down the height of two men."

He hopped down into the pit and then looked up at her. "I was going to have you come down here to see this, but I don't want to ruin your slacks."

"Don't worry about it; I want to see. Give me a hand."

With both hands, he kept her steady as she made her way down. "Sorry, I'm dirty."

For once, she didn't care about the dirt. That's how eager she was to be near him; to spend time with him. Except, he seemed to be all business as he pointed in different directions.

"My understanding is that the etching of a snake has been used several times when mapping out the destination of a treasure. Look at the head of the snake here."

"I can see it. It's definitely a snake," she said, starting to believe him.

"The head can point you in the direction you need to dig, see? If the head is crossed out or destroyed, then it means the treasure has already been found. The head here has been crossed over and since the markings don't look recent, I believe it means to stop wasting my time."

# CHAPTER 12

"Oh, I'm so sorry," Faith said, and threw her arms around Brien's neck.

Brien didn't know what to say in return, but he did like her arms around him, so he didn't speak or move. Apparently, Faith thought his lack of response meant he was upset, because she tightened her grip and he moved his arms from her shoulders to her lower back. Even though he liked this position, he stepped back because he didn't want Faith to think he was a pervert.

"I'm okay, Faith."

"You are?"

"Yes, I knew the odds were against me to find treasure, but I had fun in the looking, the reading of the signs."

"Good, I'm glad."

"But I was hoping for my family's gold. Pop had such hopes and I've been thinking about it for a long time. You know, what I'd buy."

"Huh. What did you want to buy?" she asked.

"Well, when I was a lot younger, I thought about a motorcycle."

She chuckled. "But now that you're older...what?"

"Pay off some school loans."

"You've grown into a practical man, sounds like. My dad saved a long time for my college tuition. I'm thankful he did."

Brien nodded.

"Can you help me get up out of here?" she asked him.

He pushed her up from behind, his hands steady at each side of her belt.

"I suppose you'll be filling this hole back up, huh?"

"Partially, then I'm going to check out this side over here for gold."

"Your hopes are still up? I'm a little surprised."

"A little...I need to make every effort to find it once and for all. I find it strange that there is supposed to be gold here, as well as signs of Spanish treasure. Perhaps my relatives made these carvings. You know, like some big joke for their offspring. If that's true, it's really not that funny."

She turned to head home. "I agree."

"Faith?"

"I know, I won't tell anybody."

"I know that. But I want to ask you to dinner."

"To dinner?" She put a hand to her chest, then moved it down quickly. "Where?"

"Murrayville Roadhouse. I hear the barbeque meats are good."

Faith's countenance changed, she looked sad, almost defeated, when she said, "Not this time, Brien. But thank you."

"Time's short you know," he returned.

She didn't reply, only walked forward with Roger at her heels.

Faith felt strange, something akin to frustration brewing inside. She was damned if she went out with Brien and damned if she didn't. The days ticked by and she knew she'd be sorry for saying no to him. Still, he wasn't done digging for gold and she wasn't ready to introduce him to the town. They'd both have the attention that they didn't want. Couldn't he see that? Must he put that on her? Last she heard, he wasn't ready for "a date."

What she did know was that she couldn't keep feeling frustrated about this. She went inside and changed her clothes into an old pair of jeans and the shirt she used for painting. After dressing, she pulled on her gardening boots and looked around for some sort of gloves that might protect her hands but came up empty.

"Come on Roger. We're going to see Brien again."

Roger whined then barked in excitement when he realized the direction they went.

"Brien," she called from above the hole.

He jumped; she would have too, the way she creeped up on him.

"Sorry, didn't mean to startle you."

"What's up?"

"I'm going to help you look for the gold."

"What?"

"Yeah, I'll just grab the pick here and you can help me down again."

He laughed. "You will not be bringing the pick down here. I'm not crazy, you know. I'm not ready to die."

She put a hand on her hip. "But I want to help you."

"Okay. Why don't you grab that small spade over there?" He pointed toward the trailer. "You know, a spade is a garden tool for digging."

This time she slapped a thigh. "I know. I have a garden, you know. It'll take too long with a spade. You should know that."

"I do know that, but I figure a spade will hurt less than a pick. You sure you want to help?"

"Ha. Ha. I'm bringing the pick."

"No. No. Why don't you bring that posthole digger? You can move more dirt with that."

She smiled. "Oh, you're no fun."

"I guess not. Get the digger and I'll help you down."

Faith hopped down safely, the posthole digger came with her and plunked down beside him. She glanced around like she knew what she was doing, just needed the right spot. He had to smile, she was so cute, and stepped back to watch her work.

After she plunked the tool down in front of her, a hand on both handles, she moved her hips back and forth into position, toes pointed outward. She bent her knees a couple of times and then gave her best attempt at slamming the digger into the ground. He knew it was her best effort because she made the move with a loud grunt. He looked down to see that she had pushed the digger down about a half an inch at most. After leaning forward, putting his hands on his knees and laughing, he moved up the side of the hole and grabbed the spade.

"Hey, don't laugh. I'm just getting warmed up." Yet, she smiled from ear-to-ear.

Brien handed her the spade. "You don't have to go deeper, Faith, as it's apparent that I've already gone down far enough. Just work on the side of the bank with me." He picked up his shovel, and said, "This part over here, I'm digging down to bedrock."

"Of course, you are."

"Okay, why are you here, Faith?"

"I want to be involved, I guess."

"You guess?"

She sighed. "I'm your friend, I want to *help*?" she answered with the intonation of a question.

"Huh." After a moment, he added, "Why don't you stand back and watch me dig down."

She nodded. "I'll start doing that, I guess."

There she was with the I guess again. He doubted he'd get much done before dark. Yet, he couldn't think of anyone else he'd rather be with. He was not totally sure why she was here, and those two facts made him worry for his sanity.

Faith saw him dig with purpose, watched his arm and leg muscles flex and listened to him grunt. This was probably not a good idea, she realized. Still she couldn't tear herself away.

He stopped, wiped his brow with the back of his hand, and did a double take at her. "What are you doing?"

"Watching you, like I was supposed to."

"You're staring."

"If you don't like it, then why did you ask me to do it?" she asked, the palm of her hand up.

"My mistake, I *guess*."

She decided a change of subject might be a good thing right now. "Say, have you heard from the second law firm?"

"I go in to see them in a couple of days. Why?"

"Just wondering if you decided what you're going to do come fall."

He moved close to Faith and rubbed her nose with a finger. "You've got dirt on your nose."

"Did you get it off?" she asked.

"No, made it worse." He smiled down at her.

She grinned. "Thanks for trying. I don't care about the dirt."

"Oh, yeah?" His thumb went across her cheek. "Your teeth look especially white now in comparison to your dirty face."

"Now, you're going to have to give my face a spit bath," she said.

He made a disturbing sound with his throat, obviously preparing to get enough spit to do the job.

"I'm kidding. Stop that, McGrew."

"Well, it was a good suggestion. Maybe I can lick your bottom lip."

It did sound divine, but dangerous. "I think you even have dirt on your teeth," she said.

"Can you wipe them off?" he asked, showing two full rows of teeth, white in contrast to his dirty face.

"I cannot," she answered, then snickered. "Back to my question. Did you decide what you're going to do come fall?"

He took a deep breath. "No and I feel frustrated that I can't come to terms with it."

"Have you prayed about it?"

His eyebrows furrowed. "What?"

"That might be the missing piece. From what you've said about Pops, I think he would've asked you that."

After a moment of silence, he said, "I think you may be right. It certainly can't hurt, can it?"

"No, it can only help. Even though you're not, I'm getting down to business. I'm going to get that spade and poke around in this far section here. I'll let you know when I find the gold."

"Sounds good to me."

Without looking Faith could tell that he watched her because he chuckled too much not to be. Then there was a moment of silence before she heard the bang of a shovel and the sound of earth moving.

Marty knew that Faith was at the trailer next door, as her car was parked at home, and he didn't see her out running in the woods.

Since she had visited him at the library with plans to work together on the grant project, he'd decided not to punish her. Now, however, he felt a rage of anger like a volcano erupting in his chest. Faith should know better. He had been waiting for her and he felt strongly that she had been waiting for him until recently. When she should have realized that the grant was going to bring them together at last, she didn't seem to care. Not like he did, anyway.

She'd stupidly left her front door unlocked and he walked in. He'd been in before, but only a few steps. This time he gave himself a tour of the house. He walked into her bedroom and could smell her perfume. He walked over to it and picked it up and inhaled. Next, he laid down on her bed and waited to surprise her, but then grew irritated and impatient.

On his way out, he pulled what he thought was her house key off her keyring and tested it on the front door for confirmation. He smiled as he put the key in his pocket and left the house for the woods beyond.

AFTER DIGGING AROUND FOR A WHILE, Faith gave up with a sigh. Her talents didn't lie within dirt and rocks, no matter how much she wanted to help Brien.

"It's going to be dark soon. Sorry I've wasted so much of your time, Brien."

He laid his shovel down and turned toward her. "Your company has been nice. I'm trying to appreciate the moment, since time together won't last, friend."

She moved in front of him. "Huh. How can you leave little ol' me, McGrew?"

"Life goes on, I'm afraid." He moved even closer to her.

Faith couldn't help but feel that his body language stated

something other than wanting to move on without her. Even with the possibility of getting her feelings hurt, she didn't want to step back from him. She had to think quickly. "You haven't lived until you're here in the winter. *Snowmobiling.* Can't do that in the big city."

He smiled. "I can, but I'd have to drive out of town. It'd take a while. I'm thinking you're trying to entice me to stay."

"Is that okay?" she asked in what, somehow, came out as an innocent tone of voice. That was good, because she was afraid of being rejected by using a more forward outburst.

"Oh, yeah." He'd dragged the last word out.

Sadly, she enjoyed these kinds of words from Brien. She took in a soft breath as if sucking the moment in. "I guess I don't have much to offer. As far as enticement."

"Oh, you have more to offer."

"Like what, McGrew?"

Faith started to close her eyes and pucker her lips. He laughed before waving a hand and saying, "Look around you at the forest, the beauty, the gold in them thar hills. That's enticing."

She stomped her foot, and it only missed him by a hair. Was she pouting? What else could it be? And the idea that she wanted at least a kiss, made him fill with joy. *She* made him fill with joy. Faith had that much power over him. Still, he reveled in it, smiled down at her until she smiled in return and his heart nearly burst.

"Well, it's getting dark. I'm heading back to the house." As he helped her move up the side of the hole, he said,

"Chicken."

"Maybe so, McGrew," she said. "Come on, Roger"

The first thing Faith wanted to do when she entered her house, was to wash the dirt off her body and hair, but first she made sure she locked the doors and gave Roger a treat for following her home without going back to Brien.

In her bedroom, she pulled off her shirt and noticed the bed was messy. Roger hadn't jumped on the bed for months.

"Roger, you're a silly dog. No more climbing around on my bed, got it?"

Roger stared blankly at her, then whined and took his place at the foot of the bed on the floor.

He must be a little stir crazy to do that. She'd have to get back to running after work as was their usual practice before the murder of crows.

# CHAPTER 13

Faith had given Roger a snip of bacon when she heard a knock at her door. Her heart started beating and a smile immediately followed as she thought how nice it was that Brien dropped by.

"Top of the morning, McGrew," she said as she opened the door wide.

"And the same to you, lassie." He nodded. "I wanted to let you know that I'm setting up a dry-washer on the claim. Do you know what that is?"

"Only that you can recover gold without using water. I'm a little nervous that you're telling me this though."

"No more blasting if that's what you're thinking. Nothing dangerous. I don't want to bother with any more permits to use the creek. I just want to go through the dirt I've dug up here."

She nodded.

"The dry-washing process uses the flow of air. The air flow, mechanical motion and vibration gets rid of the worthless materials. So, my point is it will be motorized and will make some noise."

"Some noise?"

"Yes, but it won't last forever. It goes through dirt pretty fast."

She pursed her lips to the side. "Then what after that?"

"Clean up the site; return the land to some semblance of order."

"Understood. It's not like you'll be working at night."

"No." After a quiet moment, he said, "Have a good day, mayor."

"Thank you, I will."

Looks like he'll be leaving sooner than later, Faith thought. If his work didn't take long, he'd probably want to move on, no reason to hang around after that. Maybe he'd move his trailer somewhere else.

What started as a happy morning, turned swiftly into a sad one. She wasn't ready for the idea of his leaving, even though she'd warned herself daily, more than once. No matter how much she wanted him around, he had other plans.

Thankfully, she had plenty to do today, to get this grant business off the ground. After she checked in at work, she'd grab a coffee and donut, then head to the library. Marty was anxious to get the work done on the front of the library, so she'd make that happen.

FAITH TOOK a napkin and wiped the donut glaze off her lips, then locked her car door and headed toward the library. She put a hand on the side of the building and looked up and over at the Victorian era storefronts with wide windows and tall doors. Lots of gray and brown paint colors had been used and crumbling bricks were sprinkled here and there. She'd like to see some different colors mixed in, as well as some canopies gracing the windows and keeping the sun out. The library would look great with window awnings, she decided.

Marty nearly ran to greet her, and his eagerness made her smile, just what she needed to perk up her sad morning.

She took his hand and shook it hard. "Well, I'm happy to see you too, Marty."

"Have you more news for me?" he asked.

"I do. I do. We've approved a company's bid to begin working on the library's storefront."

"Nice, nice. When will this happen?" he asked, still smiling.

"On Monday. That is, someone will come down and start measuring and ordering the materials that are needed."

"And I suppose you'll be here a lot, too."

Even though Faith appreciated his welcome, she decided she'd better guard her wording, not wanting him to think they'd spend any additional time together. "Not too much, Marty. I don't know much about construction, but we have a council member or two who will know what they're looking at. Bruce would be exceptionally good at this. Do you know Bruce?"

"Uh...yes, I know who that is."

She felt bad that she'd made him lose his smile, but she only told him the truth. "You certainly don't want a middle school teacher to approve anything on the library."

"I suppose not. I do understand."

But his body language told her something different. Marty went from scowling to looking angry. Perhaps he didn't care for Bruce. She'd email Bruce and ask him about this, but she couldn't think of anyone who didn't like Bruce. Especially with his keen sense of humor.

"Ok," she said. "I just want to take a few pictures of the storefront from the inside and the outside. You can come with me if you like, let me know what angle might be the best."

"Sure." He took her arm, and she tensed as he guided her to the front. To get the right angle, he put his hands on her shoulders and with a hand, he moved her face just so.

"Thank you, that should work for inside," she said. "I will go myself and take several of the front, that way I will have every angle."

He nodded, and she could feel his gaze on her as she walked outside. As she moved her cell phone to take aim for a good shot, she spotted Marty staring at her from the inside of the library, far enough back that he wouldn't be in the picture. Most would probably say that he only made sure the library's position was well taken care of, but the hairs rising on her arms told her this was something altogether different. The next time she came to visit, she would bring someone with her, so she didn't inadvertently encourage him in any way.

BRIEN SHOVELED dirt into the dry-washer but his thoughts were on Faith. She'd puckered up for a kiss last night, and he played the gentleman and didn't kiss her back. What was the matter with him? He was crazy, that's the matter. Any other girl… Yes, that had to be it. Faith was a beauty but didn't seem to know it. And she was kind and giving, so much so that this town was lucky to have her working on its behalf. Because of what she was, he wouldn't…no, he couldn't take advantage of her. Yet, not because of her, but because of him. If his heart grew one iota fonder of her, he'd end up working on some high-rise building looking out the window with a broken heart.

He knew she had feelings for him, yet she didn't ask him

to stay, to work here. That was the kind of person she was. The last thing she'd do is tell him what to do; what job to take. She wouldn't give him an answer even if he asked her opinion.

Too bad, because he could use the help deciding.

Faith was right when she said to pray about it, and then listen. He'd already prayed about it some. Not that he'd hear His voice, but he could watch what happened in his life and decide from there.

He stopped working then, deciding to make a sandwich and eat outside under a big pine tree to pray and think. That kind of behavior sure couldn't hurt.

FAITH LEFT WORK A LITTLE EARLY, anxious to hear just how much noise Brien's dry-washer could make. *As if.* Pity, he was all she thought of, but that was the way it was.

At home, she stepped out of her car and could hear the dry-washer in motion. After getting the mail, she went through the keys on her keyring, but couldn't find the front door key. Three instances she looked, then stopped to think what could've happened. The last time she'd used it, was after work yesterday. She knew she hadn't given it to anyone. After opening her wallet, she checked to see if anyone took her credit cards. No, they were still there.

She sat down on the porch steps and considered when she'd been without her purse. Only after work yesterday until this morning when she left the house. This was beyond weird. Perhaps it fell loose and dropped into her purse. She stood, then dumped the whole thing on the sidewalk and picked up one item at a time and placed it back in her purse. It wasn't there. She didn't know whether to be alarmed or not, but her heart started pounding anyway.

Yet, what would someone want with her key? She snapped her purse shut and walked over to the rock at the side of the house, where her father had left a spare key. It was there, at least she could get into the house.

But did she *want* to go in the house? What if someone was there, or someone had robbed her. This was crazy, of course she could enter the house.

After releasing Roger from his crate, he followed her to the front door, with a swinging tail and little whimpers of joy. The first thing she did was to give him a doggie biscuit from a container on a shelf near the door. Afterwards, she patted her thigh for him to follow her around the house. He seemed fine, like nothing untoward had happened in the house, until they walked in her bedroom and he slowly sniffed around the bed. When he lifted his head and looked at the bed, her heart dipped in fear. Yet, since Roger didn't seem to think that anyone was in the room, she approached the closet and slowly opened the door. Roger watched her as if in interest, but then barreled down the stairs.

Roger was right, there was no one there under her clothes or in the corners. She let out a loud sigh. Still, she turned to look at the bed once more. The spread wasn't disheveled, like it was last evening when Roger had hopped on the bed. Faith shook her head, as she couldn't think of anyone who would want to enter her house like this, and there had to be some other simple answer to what happened to her key.

Most likely, one of her middle school students got into her purse and took her key. *Ha, ha.* Very funny. "Just wait until I get ahold of you, kid."

Downstairs, Faith opened the door for Roger to go out. She couldn't hear the dry-washer anymore, but she did see Brien leave in his truck. Her heart fell again, not due to fear but disappointment. He had her hook, line and sinker and there was nothing she could do about it.

THE NEXT AFTERNOON, Faith offered a reward to her fourth, fifth and sixth period classes. She declared that she'd lost a key somewhere. Two girls came forward and looked around her desk, and one boy came back after school to look around the room, besides that, no one had a clue. No body language gave anything sinister away.

She reported her loss to the lost and found department, so she'd covered her bases at school.

At home, Brien had not returned, and she remembered that he said he had another meeting with the other law firm coming up. She hoped he would call and let her know how it went, but why would he? They were not that close. It was not like she told him about the council meetings she'd attended. No, that would be awkward and drive him away if nothing else.

Still, she wrote Brien a note stressing that she wanted to know how the interview went. Roger led the way to his trailer where Faith left the note on his screen door. That way, she didn't have to listen for him to come back to his trailer because the note let him know she wanted to hear from him.

MARTY STOOD in the dark watching Faith from afar. He'd turned off his flashlight and crossed his arms as he enjoyed a nice viewpoint of her in the kitchen, apparently washing dishes in the sink. Her lips moved as if singing a song, her head jerked to the beat, and then her arms went over her head in a slow stretch before she started singing again. He wondered what song it was and if he would like it too. Most likely, as he couldn't help but love everything about her.

He straightened and wondered if he should go in the

house, surprise her. But then, her stupid dog started barking and moved him out of his amorous thoughts. He didn't want her to call the police, nor did he want to get bit by her dog if he came out the door after him. Slowly, he moved toward the trailer and the dog stopped barking.

He walker closer to the dark trailer and saw a white piece of paper on the door. Drawing nearer, he took the paper and shined his flashlight on it. Faith had signed it and she'd invited him to come and see her.

Anger filled him as he considered her recklessness. He covered his mouth, not wanting to curse out loud and alert the dog again. Instead, he rumpled the paper and put it in his pocket.

Next, he walked over to the large hole the man had dug and saw a dry-washer alongside. He snorted. What an idiot, he thought. There was a creek less than a mile away. No, he didn't need a dry-washer when using water was a better way to go.

Being a miner himself, Marty didn't understand the mess this man had made. He dug a hole deep and wide enough to bury a body. Which gave him an idea...

For now, though he'd make his presence known. He went over to the dry-washer and turned it over.

The stupid dog started barking again, so he hightailed it over to where he'd parked his truck, hopped inside and laughed hard and loud. He loved it when a plan came together in his mind.

FAITH HAD HOPED that Roger's barking had to do with Brien, but his growling and the fierceness of his bark told her this wasn't Brien coming home. She closed every window blind in the house and made sure the dead bolts were utilized in both doors. She was more than relieved when Roger finally calmed down for good.

In the morning, she'd go see her friend Holly. Having a detective friend gave her the feeling of calm that she needed to get through the quiet evening that followed.

## CHAPTER 14

"Holly, do you have a minute?" Faith asked.

Detective Holly Mason stood up from her desk and straightened her skirt with a hand. "I have a few minutes. What's up? Having problems with your neighbor again? Attorney… What's his name?" she asked and laughed.

Faith put a hand on her hip. "Ha. Ha. No, it's something else I'm worried about."

Holly stopped smiling. "Okay, go ahead."

Knowing Holly had limited time, she spoke quickly ending with Roger barking last night.

She sat on the edge of her desk. "You know that dogs bark for various reasons."

"Of course, I do. But Roger acted differently this time."

"He could have gotten a whiff of a coyote or bear."

"Yes, you're right, Holly. It could have been something like that. I hadn't thought about another animal."

"Bears have been spotted in your area, Faith." After a moment, she added, "Do you think your father could have taken the key off your key ring when he was in town?"

"No, because I had the key to open my door the day before it went missing."

"It seems logical that the key slipped off the ring and it's lying around somewhere. You wouldn't have heard it if it had dropped onto a carpet."

"I'll look again. Thanks, Holly. I feel better."

"One last question concerning the murder of crows and the rock that spun out and hit you. Do you have any reason to think that someone might be following you around?"

"Actually, the rock didn't spin out from the crows. It came at me from a different direction. I can't explain how it hit really, I just know it did." Faith looked out the window at the flowers in the distance, then shook her head. "I don't know of anyone that would do something like this, Holly."

"You were relaxed and then you tensed up again. I don't want to worry you, Faith, I just want you to pay attention to your surroundings. You should be aware of your surroundings anyway. You should get your locks changed." Holly straightened before saying, "If you think of anything else, let me know. Got to go."

"Okay. Thanks. I'll see you around town."

Holly nodded, grabbed her phone, put it in her suit pocket, and went down the hall in front of her.

BACK IN HER OFFICE, Faith went through her mail. By the color of an envelope, someone had sent her a card. She smiled, thinking it was nice to be appreciated. People didn't send very many thank you cards anymore. On second thought, it didn't have a return address and could very well be a business advertisement. She took the letter opener from her desk and opened it. The front of the card said *Thinking of You*, the inside was blank, yet a short note scribed in neat printing, no name listed. *To my dear Faith,* she read, *I have watched you from afar, but that will soon change. Get ready to welcome me, for you are my soulmate. Fate can wait no longer. Sincerely, Your Secret Admirer.*

Faith shook her head. "Oh, no. Oh, no." *This can't be happening. No, no.* She put her head in her hands, and something in her stomach hardened, leaving her feeling like she'd been hit.

She opened her laptop and left an email for Holly, then found the number of a locksmith. She wasn't going home without one.

~

FAITH USED a credit card to pay for the locksmith and then took the new keys he handed her. She watched him get in his truck and leave, making her feel very alone.

Roger whined and she patted his head. "You're a good boy, Roger. I'm going to really depend on your company for a while."

She walked over to the window and looked out toward the trailer. She'd not seen any sign of Brien, but she didn't need to look for him, as she'd left a note on his door. Instead, she closed the blinds no matter that the sun had yet to set.

Faith heard a vehicle. She peeked out a blind and saw Brien pulling in toward his trailer. She took a deep breath and then let it out in a rush. At least someone was nearby.

An hour went by and he still hadn't come over. She told herself that he probably needed some rest after the trip to Portland and the important job interview. He'd come when he could.

This was the first time she'd felt so alone in this house. For comfort, Faith wrapped her arms around herself and then rubbed her arms. She lay down on the couch to rest and wait for Brien. In the middle of the night, she jerked awake trying to scream. "Breathe in, breathe out," she told herself.

Roger nosed her forehead, before she stood and arched her back. "Come on. Let's go up to bed, Roger."

~

THE FOLLOWING DAY started as usual for Faith. The dark night had turned to a sunlit day and light spilled in through her kitchen window. At the moment, the fear she experienced yesterday was at bay. It also helped that Brien was next door.

After breakfast, Roger barked at the front door, dispelling her decent mood. She rubbed her arms while she tried to decide whether she should hide and ignore what this could mean or go to the window and look out like a normal person.

After a knock on the door, Roger's ferocious bark turned into a playful yip and whine. Just as he'd always done when Brien stood on the porch. It was logical that Brien would come over, this was not the first time he'd come over before she left for work.

She swung the door open wide. "Hello, Brien. I see you got my note."

"Hi. What note?"

"The one I left on your door, telling you to come over."

"I didn't see one. I was wondering if we had some strong winds when I was out of town."

"No. I don't think so."

He scratched his head. "Well, obviously the note blew away and then the dry-washer was turned over."

"Huh. Is it damaged?"

"No, doesn't look like it. It's just odd is all. It would have to be a very hard wind to topple it with the way I had it braced up."

"There was someone out there night before last. Roger couldn't stop barking."

"Any cars parked out front?"

"No. That was the first thing I looked for. I'm glad you're back."

"Scared you, huh?"

"Well, that and my house key was missing?"

"Did you find it?"

"No. And I got a weird letter from a secret admirer."

"It wasn't me," he said, hand on chest.

"No, I didn't think it was you. Anyway, I changed my locks."

"Probably a good thing to do." He sat down. "Can I see the letter?"

"Sure." She pulled it from her purse and handed it to him.

"That is rather creepy," he said, looking up.

"I am keeping my detective friend in the loop. Maybe it was just some letter someone sent…upset about something political, but I can't think of any issues at hand."

"You are a pretty woman."

"Thanks…I guess." After a moment, she said, "Enough about me. How did your interview go?"

"I didn't take the job."

"Oh. Are you taking the other one, then?"

"No, not that one either."

"Let me get something to drink, because you need to explain." She turned toward the kitchen without waiting for a reply and Brien followed behind her.

"I don't want to bore you."

"Coffee, tea or lemonade?"

"Lemonade."

Faith filled two glasses with ice and set them on the

counter. "Believe me, you won't. I find it very interesting that you turned down two formidable firms."

Brien watched her fill the glasses with a pitcher of lemonade. "What? Are you disappointed I didn't take a job with lots of pay, no choice of clients and with a very good chance of hardening my conscience and damaging my life in the process?"

"Well, if you put it that way. Yet, I can see why the decision was hard. Most people would probably go for the glory."

"Yes, I think they would. Both firms looked at me like I was crazy when I turned them down."

"So now what?"

He sipped his lemonade before sitting down at the kitchen table. "You were right to tell me to consider what Pops would have told me—to pray about this."

Faith took a seat as well. "That's the best advice I can think of."

He nodded. "I've been thinking back to what I always wanted to do; help those who can't help themselves, you know?"

She rotated her glass and the ice clinked. "Not much money there, though."

"That's right, so I'll have to do something else, too. But it will be my choice. I suppose I can even teach law. My strength is semantics. Laws have, or need, to be plainly clear and people need to have the answers. Not understanding the law has never been an excuse that works. Anyway, I can look at the words in a law and figure them out faster than some."

"I'll take your glass, Brien. I'll set them in the sink for now."

"Okay, thanks."

She turned toward him, crossed her arms and smiled. "By-the-way, many elected bureaucrats are lawyers and they are known to work with the semantics of words."

"Yes, but I'm not talking about changing words around to prove my point as some do, my dear."

"Whew," she said and pretended to wipe her brow with the back of her hand.

"You have a beautiful smile," he said. After a moment of staring at her lips, he added, "Now tell more about the key you lost."

She stood, her smile turning into a frown. "That's just it. I don't think I lost it. After the evening I was with you digging, I came home and prepared to end the day as usual. Now, I had left the door unlocked since I was just going to see you. When I came back nothing was amiss, except the bedspread on my bed was messed up, but I thought maybe Roger had done it. He used to do it, anyway, but it had been awhile.

"The next day, when I came home, I looked for my key on my key ring to open the door and it was missing. I didn't take it off; I had had it the day before when I came home from work. Before you say anything, it was not in the bottom of my purse or on the floor anywhere. No one at work or school had seen it."

Brien walked into the living room and then turned around. "I didn't take it. I want you to know that."

"I know that. If you wanted something, you'd be direct. You wouldn't sneak around about it."

"Thanks for your vote of confidence." He sat down on the couch. "So, the note you wrote to me has vanished, you got a letter, your key is missing, and my dry-washer was turned over. Not much to build a case on, but it's enough to pay attention to."

She nodded her head.

"I'll keep an eye out for you. And you should probably move around town with someone else. Not alone."

"I will."

# CHAPTER 15

*B*rien watched Faith get in her car and leave for work. After he put a hand out to wave good-bye, he turned to look at the dry-washer that he'd only now righted. Yet, his thoughts were on Faith. He never did like that she lived out here alone most of the time, and he hated the idea now.

Somehow, he needed to convince her that she needed to move closer into town. Perhaps he could convince her...but then it wasn't any of his business. He had his own whereabouts to deal with.

By the end of the day, he'd probably be done shoveling the rest of the dirt and rocks through the dry-washer and then he could return it to the business he'd rented it from in town.

He took his concern and frustration over Faith's safety, turned it into energy and began shoveling. That is until he saw a blob of dirt hit the washer but didn't break up. He turned off the machine and picked the thing up.

~

FAITH MET Rose Langley and Marty Walker at her office door. "Hello, Marty and Rose. You're early, Rose." Faith turned the key and opened the door.

"I am. I have a doctor's appointment later. Won't let me change the time," she said, and her body language told Faith that she wasn't happy about that.

She set down a file and her bag on the desk, then touched Rose's shoulder. "Don't worry about it, Rose. I'll take you anytime I can get you."

Rose had apparently dismissed her problem, as she turned to Marty and said, "Now, what brings you here, Marty? Are you here to see our girl?"

"I am the mayor, not anybody's girl."

"Well, yes," said Marty. "I thought I'd stop by on the way to work and make an appointment for when you are going to come back by the library. You know, concerning the grant."

"Well, thanks for the reminder. I've had a lot on my mind recently, so your presence is helpful. I have to check with a few people and then I'll let you know."

"How will you let me know? I suppose I can meet you somewhere if need be."

"Oh, no, no. I'll call. Thanks for stopping by, Marty."

Marty stood there with his mouth open for a moment and then said, "Okay. Until then." He nodded then turned out the door.

"That was almost cold, Faith," said Rose.

"Well, I didn't mean to sound cold. I hadn't expected to see either of you here. Caught me off guard is all."

"I suppose he is interested in getting the library fixed up. Or, he could be here because you are a single, attractive woman."

"Oh, please don't go there. I'm not interested in him. I've been nothing but professional around him. You know, friendly is all."

"Well, men sometimes take friendly differently. Especially since he's a widower. He had no choice in losing his wife."

She hoped not. For a moment, she wondered if Marty could be the secret admirer, but considered him harmless.

"I need you to file these files right here. I've saved them for you."

"Okay," said Rose and let out a breath that sounded like some sort of defeat. "I'll see if I can remember alphabetical order."

Faith chuckled at that, as it was beyond Rose to mess anything up. She just so wanted her matched up to somebody. Well, she did too, but the one she wanted she couldn't have.

MARTY WAS SO SEETHED with anger that he could barely focus on his way to the library. He was far less than happy to be sent away as abruptly as he'd been by Faith. Especially since he'd spent so much time on her. Thinking of her, planning for her and watching her.

The moment he sat down at his desk at the library, he took out a piece of paper and wrote her an anonymous letter of warning. Afterwards, he put it in a desk drawer to look at after work. He may have something to add after a day of thinking. Yet, the main idea would stay the same: Damage Faith Chadwick's reputation.

Maybe he shouldn't send her a letter, just start spreading the word at Murrayville Roadhouse. In this small town, everyone knew that she hated this type of publicity. Once his mind steadied, he changed his mind. No, he'd send her a letter. She had to know that he had done this to her credibility.

Yet, if he had to be honest, she was doing this to herself

with that man next door. He doubted a man who lived in a small trailer looking for gold would stay around for the long haul with Faith. But he'd be there to help her lick her wounds when the man left, or when he died, he didn't know which. He had more to think about.

FAITH COULDN'T WAIT to get home and see Brien. She knew it was stupid to feel that way, but she couldn't help the fond feelings that welled up in her chest. She told herself that she felt safer with him around.

She hurried to her car and saw a paper under the windshield wiper. That was strange, she thought. It wasn't as if it was a business advertisement. No, it was a sheet of paper from a yellow legal pad. After getting inside her car, she set her bag down and put the keys in the ignition but wouldn't start the car until she had a chance to read the paper.

All fond feelings vanished as she opened the letter and saw the same handwriting that was on the secret admirer note. Instantly, she pushed a button on the door to lock herself in. Fear gripped her and she put a hand at her chest. "Help me, God. *Help me*."

She forced herself to calm down and focus on the threats contained in the letter. She couldn't think of what she'd done to deserve this and then wondered if she should go to see Holly. Instead, she decided to take a picture of the letter and send it to her by phone.

Through the car windows, Faith looked around outside and didn't see anyone she knew, except for Marty talking to someone in front of the library.

I hope Brien is at his claim, she thought and started the car.

～

BRIEN HEARD the engine of a car, so he moved to the space in the woods where he could see and not be seen. He thought he'd been done with the hiding stuff, but after Faith's admirer had made himself known, he thought he would continue to be out of sight.

His heart warmed to see Faith pass by and drive into her driveway. He'd been feeling like a silly lovesick boy and it was worse today.

As he walked toward her, he saw a frown on her face as she took the mail out of the mailbox. Nothing good happened today, apparently. She looked up, startled at first, and then shock turned into a wide smile.

"Top o' the evenin' to ya," he said with an Irish lilt.

"Top o' the evenin' to you, too, but it's not yet evening."

"Aye, just planning ahead."

She nodded, smiling.

He had her smiling, and he didn't want her any other way. Ever. "Let's get Roger out here. Then you can tell me about your day."

The smile vanished. "Okay."

He took the key from her hand and walked in front of her.

"Does anything in here look disturbed to you?" he asked her.

She walked around then stopped and looked up the stairs. After she stood there for a moment, he let Roger out and took a treat from a box, gave it to him and let him out the front door.

"Thanks Brien." She turned toward him.

After she told him about the new note, he moved forward and said, "Come with me and we'll check out the upstairs. Just to be sure no one has been in here today. Let me go first."

"Okay."

They entered her bedroom last and when he stopped, she moved right up against him.

"I didn't realize that the note, now notes, had disturbed you so." He turned toward her and took her hands in his."Yeah, I didn't realize it either, until the last note and now coming into the house again."

"Does everything look okay in here?"

After a moment, she added, "Everything looks fine."

"Good. As much as I'd like to stay in this room, I don't want to take advantage of you when you've been upset." Still, he wiggled his eyebrows.

She chuckled. "You mean, you don't want me to take advantage of you."

"Oh, yes, there's that. My fragile psyche could not take it."

He loved that he could make her laugh, too. Music to his ears as he'd been concerned about her.

At the bottom of the stairs, he took her hand and lead her to the front porch and out in the yard. Roger ran circles around them, happy to be loose and with them.

It was hard not to laugh at Roger, his excitement was so abundant. Brien let the antics of the dog move over him and happiness filled him. He wanted this dog and this woman. He pulled her to him from behind and she laid her head back on him and watched Roger, too.

"Okay, now that Roger has helped brighten the day, I want you to tell me what the letter said. What kind of threats did he make?"

"It seems that this person is assuming I am aware of some things that I have no way of knowing. Somehow, I'm not expressing my love for him, when I'm not expressing anything to anyone these days."

"Maybe a little bit to me, though, huh?"

"I suppose so. But we've already assumed this fellow isn't you, right?"

"Ha. Ha. Now, what else?"

"I know you are just trying to cheer me up, McGrew."

"So, shoot me. Now what else?"

"Apparently, somehow I have rejected him and if I continue to do so, then he will ruin my reputation in this town."

"He seems to know you enough to know that that's something you don't want. That's your number one fear, I'm thinking."

She sighed. "Yes, it has been."

"Do other people know this too? Have you expressed this to anyone else?"

Faith thought for a moment, then answered, "I have told those that want to play matchmaker that I'm not interested in having a relationship scrutinized by the town."

Brien nodded.

"But now with this scary secret admirer thing, it all seems so stupid."

"Well, you had some bad boyfriends."

"That's what everyone says, and I believe it now."

"Have you expressed these views with a man? Has anyone been close enough that you could share these things with him?"

She shook her head. "I don't think so. We can go back inside and get the note so you can see it."

"In a minute, I want you to come to the claim with me. I have something to show you."

"Sure. A change of subject is good."

The first thing that Faith noticed was that the hole was almost all filled. He'd be done soon, she realized, and the idea didn't lift her spirits any. "Looks like you will be done soon."

"Well, I've put just about everything through the dry-washer and I want to show you the flakes I've found.

"Oh, good, Brien! Why didn't you tell me that when you first came over?"

"Because, you seemed to have something on your mind."

"Let me see the gold."

"Don't get your hopes up. It's not as much as I'd hoped for."

Brien unlocked the trailer door and stepped inside. He brought out a gold pan with enough flakes to nearly cover half the bottom circle.

"Good, that's good."

"Yes, it is, but gold mining is a hard way to make a living. It was fun seeing these flakes, but my days of mining are about over. Still, I have something else to show you."

"Oh, okay."

He took the pan inside the trailer and brought back a two-cup sized bowl. "Before you look, feel the weight."

She closed her eyes and he placed the bowl in her hands. "More weight than I thought I'd be lifting. Can I look now?"

"Sure."

She didn't quite know what this was, but it was dirty. "What…"

He took the bowl from her and held it between them. "I shoveled dirt into the dry-washer. I saw this blob of dirt, and I hit it with the shovel to try and break it up, but it was awkward, didn't move or come apart like all the rest. I turned the washer off and picked it up."

"What is it?" she asked.

"Well, look." He moved the object enough so she could see a gold color."

"That's the color of gold…"

"It is gold, my dear Faith." He put the bowl back into her

hands. "What's partially around the gold, is an old tanned leather bag that has been decomposing over the years."

"There's hardly any shape left to the bag." She saw that the gold nuggets varied in size.

"Yeah, I didn't see it when I dug down. I feel very blessed that I found it now."

"So, is this the treasure or the family's gold?"

"Good question." He looked up to the top of the trees and then back down at her. "The only thing I know is that if it was Spanish treasure then the leather would have disintegrated by now. I'm not even sure if this is the Harney County gold, because that bag would have totally decomposed by now, too."

She nodded. "Do you think you have very much here, Brien?"

"You mean value?"

"Yeah."

"It's about two and a half pounds, I think. So, according to the calculator on my phone, that would be a value of around $406,000."

# CHAPTER 16

"*W*ow, Brien. Wow… Wow."

"Yes, I know. There was a hopeful part of me that thought I might be able to find some gold, but I had given up on the notion that it'd happen. Gold *or* treasure."

"Wow," she said again. "Do you think Pops could have planted this?"

His eyes teared up. "That's the only thing that makes any kind of sense."

"What do you mean?"

"Pops always talked about going back to this site. I think he'd given up on the family gold and that he made the symbols, carved them. Perhaps he'd finally given up on my going with him, but he always talked about finding gold someday and paying off my student loans. The last thing he said to me was to go find the gold. After his death, a note to me had a hand drawn map and GPS coordinates."

"Yes, it all adds up, doesn't it?"

He nodded. "He was a gold miner and had accumulated some gold over the years, looks like." After a moment, he shook his head as if to clear it and said, "I must ask. Does this gold make me sexier?"

Faith smiled from ear-to-ear. "Yes, it helps."

"Well, good to know."

She laughed out loud.

"I'd also like to know, if you'd go with me to Murrayville Roadhouse. Dinner and maybe a dance."

The question sobered her good mood and she frowned.

"It's just dinner. Your reputation will be ruined anyway, sounds like. Besides, you really don't need to go anywhere alone for a while. Not until this stalker thing is figured out."

"Don't say it like that. That's not a special invitation at all." She smiled, belying the seriousness of her words.

He gave her a half smile. "Okay." After clearing his throat, he said, "I'm interested in you. Will you go with me to the Roadhouse tonight?"

She put her hand on her chest and batted her eyelashes. "Well, I didn't know you were interested in me, Brien. I would be honored to go out with you tonight."

He let out something between a chortle and a guffaw, but it was filled with joy.

Faith skipped on her way back to the house, so he figured they both felt the same way.

The minute Faith entered the house, she grabbed her phone and called Rose Langley. Her hello sounded a bit perturbed to be bothered, but she lightened right up when Faith told her who she was, and that she had a date and would be at the roadhouse tonight.

Not that Faith wanted trouble, but she didn't want to be scared anymore. Not about her secret admirer and not about hiding her private life. Besides, it was high time she moved on with her life.

FAITH LOOKED through her closet and came up with jeans, a dressy pink blouse and high heel sandals. That was about as dressed up as would be suitable for the roadhouse.

The band Murrayville Outlaws played at the roadhouse and she was happy about that. She'd not been on a date in a long time and she welcomed the idea of a fun night with loud music and lots of boot stomping.

While she waited for Brien her hands started to shake. Even though she was finally going out with someone she really wanted to date, she had a stalker who'd be watching her along with the rest of the town. She'd be on display tonight, any way she looked at it.

While Brien would soon leave town, she had to live up to this night of exposure, whatever it may bring. She wished she could just enjoy Brien's arms before he went away and it could only help to have the stalker see them together. Besides, the stalker hadn't yet acted out on his fantasies and hopefully he wouldn't after he saw her interest in someone else.

Naïve, maybe, but she believed she had to be way too young to stop enjoying her life.

BRIEN LOOKED good in a blue-green t-shirt and black slim-fit cargo pants. The five o'clock shadow that graced his chin in the back woods was gone, leaving a bare square chin. Perhaps he planned to go cheek-to-cheek, she thought, and felt her face redden.

"You okay?" he asked.

"Yes. You look good is all." She turned away as she'd suddenly wanted to hide her feelings. "Roger, let's get you some food." She walked to the kitchen and opened the pantry. "I'll only be a minute. I forgot all about Roger. He needs to eat something in case I get home late."

"*Will* you be returning home late?" He teased her now, but she couldn't help but smile.

"I'll see if my date is a dud or not. Here you go, big boy."

Roger nearly inhaled his food, then drank about half of a large dog bowl of water, drops of spilling out around him. She opened the back door and Roger barreled out nearly knocking her over to get out the door.

"Are you okay?" he asked and reached out a hand toward her.

"Are you kidding? I'm used to this dog manhandling me. I just brace myself and close my eyes and I do okay," she said while toweling up the spilled water.

"Makes life worth living, huh?"

"It sure does. He makes my life so much better."

"Yeah, I miss having a dog."

She pushed a lock of hair behind her ear. "You'll get settled one of these days."

He smiled, but his thoughts abruptly seemed distant.

Roger ran back in to Brien and he rubbed his head.

"I think I will just leave him loose in the house tonight. He had some time in his crate earlier."

He nodded.

"Okay, let's go then."

Faith held onto his collar as Brien left the house and then she backed out with the palm of her hand at Roger's nose. "There," she said, with her back to the closed door.

They walked over to Brien's truck and he opened the passenger door for her. She hopped up and scooted in.

On the trip to town, Brien noted that Faith nervously placed her thumbs side by side as if to measure them between bouts of turning her knuckles inward.

Brien pulled into the Murrayville Roadhouse parking lot,

parked and took the keys. "Are you uncomfortable around me, or something?"

"What?" She looked down at her hands. "No. I've just had a lot on my mind."

He reached over her and pushed open her door. "I hope I'm one of them."

"I like your aftershave."

When she didn't answer his question, he said, "Well, at least I don't stink."

"Yes, I've thought about you," she finally said. "Hard not to think about you. You *know* I think about you."

"I just needed to hear it, I guess."

Faith wanted to ask him if he thought about her but hopped out of the truck instead. The parking lot full of cars moved her thoughts to the anxious heart beating in her chest. Because of dread, she froze in place.

"So, there are a lot of people here. That's okay. You've done nothing to be ashamed of, Faith. We're here to have fun. Introduce me to a few people and you'll give me that dance you promised."

She turned to look at him. "I promised you a dance, didn't I?"

"There, that's the way to be. Come on. I hear the band has started."

"Yes, I hear it too," she said, excited at the sound of the bass guitar but still a feeling of unease following her.

He took her hand. "I bet you haven't danced in a long time."

She tightened the grip on his hand. "You'd be right. Okay, let's go in."

As they walked in, it took a moment for her eyes to adjust to the darkness. Couples were on the dance floor, moving to a fast beat of a song she knew. The band was known to play classic rock.

"Brien, I'd like you to meet my friend and detective, Holly Mason. Holly this is Brien McGrew."

Brien shot out a hand in greeting. "It's nice to have a face with a name, detective."

"Call me Holly, Brien."

"Okay, I will, Holly."

Rose sat at the bar but swiveled to face them. "Brien, over here. This is my friend and the mayor's right-hand gal, Rose Langley. Rose this is Brien McGrew."

"How do you do, Brien. So, are you Faith's date tonight?"

"I am, Ms. Langley."

"Oh, my. You are a handsome thing," she said. "Call me Rose, please."

"Thank you, Rose." He kissed the back of her hand and bowed.

Rose smiled demurely, affected by a handsome man, Faith noted and chuckled.

"I'm counting on you to take good care with Faith, here. She's a fine woman."

"Yes, she is, and I will be good to her, you can count on that."

Rose winked at Faith and she chuckled again. Marty Walker sat down beside Faith and she nodded to him before turning to introduce Brien to councilman Bruce and his wife Gail. She felt good about taking Brien out of the woods, literally, and including her friends in her life with Brien, no matter how limited their relationship may prove to be.

"Do you want to get something to eat?" Brien asked her as the song ended.

She looked around. "Not yet. Let's dance first. I'm not ready to be interrupted yet, you know?"

"Uh, yes. Famous in Murrayville."

"*What*? I'm just anxious to dance with you, McGrew."

"Sure," Brien said in a sarcastic tone and once on the

dance floor moved her so that her back was to the crowd and she appreciated the gesture.

He, however, looked out above her head and made his back ramrod straight as if his mother was watching. She'd have to change that by making him look at her.

The song the Outlaws played changed beats from fast to slow, but Faith managed to move to a little of both rhythms while he watched her rather than dance.

"Move. Don't just stand there, McGrew."

He mimicked disco moves, starting with a pointed index finger moving up and then down across his body and she stopped dancing to laugh at him.

The band picked up the beat and she danced around him moving her face close to his when she was near enough, then moved back and away. As the song ended, she danced to him and put her arms around his shoulders. She returned an ample smile that made her know without a doubt that he thought of her as someone special. She remembered that he'd told her that she was attractive and intelligent and that she had accomplished a lot in her young life.

Faith realized she didn't need to have her back to the crowd because at this moment, she only had eyes for Brien.

# CHAPTER 17

*B*rien thoroughly enjoyed watching Faith's hips sway from side to side as she had danced around him and that he'd like to blot her shiny lipstick with his mouth.

Had he not realized how drop dead sexy she was until this moment? No, he knew, but realized the undivided attention she gave him now put on a show for not only her secret admirer but the city's patrons as well.

A slow dance gifted him with her arms back around his shoulders and her head settled on his chest. He took in the coconut scent of her hair that smelled even better than the sweetest flower.

She looked up at him and smiled a smile that gave him a small electrical charge that went halfway down his body. She'd done it before, again with only a smile. This type of jolt, he'd never experienced with any other woman, and he found it hard to return the smile without causing a fire.

Time seemed to stand still until the band cranked up the beat again. Obviously, this was a favorite song of hers, because she bent, pulled off her sandals and sent them flying along the floor to the back wall. Faith closed her eyes and lifted her arms and half swayed them and half snapped her fingers as she turned in a circle, then danced with her knees and feet for all she was worth.

This girl was magical with him. How could he let her go? He tried to calm his thoughts by attempting to do a moon walk but nearly fell over the lady behind him. It helped center his thoughts, however.

Faith was in her own world, eyes closed and slowly spinning to the music. He smiled; he was glad that he could give her this night. Her behavior let him know that this event was long overdue, and he wondered what she'd do if he returned to Portland. He noticed the *if* in his thoughts for the very first time.

Brien stood in the same place and slowly moved his elbows and knees while he watched Faith. She'd just moved forward dipped her head and then threw her blonde hair back over her shoulders.

He started to feel like a smitten schoolgirl as he wondered if she'd still care about him if he went home. Would she remember what he considered a magical night to be only just another uh...date? She could hurt him, he suddenly learned.

Brien wanted—no needed—to be sure of her. He wanted to be her treasure. Here he was nearly a big shot attorney so sure of himself but feared rejection from this little gal. *Ha.*

After he made a wish that this enchanted night would last, he pulled her into her his arms and danced slowly, no matter the lively beat of the music, because she was his tonight and he wanted to appreciate the moment. Oh, my goodness, Brien thought and sighed in her ear.

The music was loud, so Faith wondered if he really made that satisfied sound, or did she only wish it to be? Then he sighed again. She pulled back and searched his face in hopes that she could read the expression. "What are you doing, McGrew?"

"Enjoying the moment." He put his hands on her face and pulled her to him. His lips opened slightly as he pressed a kiss on her lips. In front of everyone, she thought, before slowly pulling back and looking up at him again.

Faith looked toward the roadhouse patrons and caught Bruce's surprised, wide-eyed look, not a frown or a warning. But she took it as such. No matter how much she liked that Brien kissed her, she did have to keep some things private from the townspeople.

Faith hoped Brien wouldn't take her movements as rejection as she put one hand on his shoulder and the other in his hand and stepped back. "Let's waltz. I've always wanted to do that."

They waltzed to a corner area where they wouldn't trample too many people.

"I'm sorry," he said, frowning and sounding hurt.

"No, don't be. I loved it. I'm hoping for more later."

"Really?" He smiled brightly and she immediately thought she needed to be careful. If he planned to leave her, as she'd always thought, she'd remember this night always. Sadly, she'd probably wonder what he was doing every minute of every day. One could only hope that the gold he found would cause him to linger and not rush back and look for a job.

Right now, Faith felt like a princess and even though she knew she needed to start bucking up, harden her emotions, uh…not…just…yet. She'd let every good feeling rush over every cell in her body before he left town.

Certainly, Faith had confidence in herself and her accomplishments, but still she was merely a small-town girl in many ways. Oh, she wanted to ask this man many questions, but didn't know if she could take the answers. Think positive thoughts, she told herself at length.

A slow dance brought her closer to him once again and she took in his handsome face, his golden-brown eyes, then she closed her eyes and took in his touch and smell for all she was worth.

At the end of the song, he said, "Even though I really like dancing with you, we need to get something to eat and drink. It can be to go, if you'd like. It's up to you."

"Yes. I'd like it to go. We can eat it in the truck."

He nodded. "I'd like to eat alone, too."

Faith told him what she wanted and then went in search of her shoes. Even though she spent time looking all around the dance floor and band, she didn't find her sandals. Dang, she loved that pair. In the case of confusion, Faith told the manager what to look for and gave him her cell number.

BRIEN PARKED his truck down the way along Main Street and passed out the food.

Faith spent time looking more at Brien than her food. She watched his jaw muscle bunch as he chewed and noticed he had great hands with long fingers and well-manicured nails. She smiled thinking he must have taken extra care to brush the dirt out of his nails for their date. Her own nervous hands played with the fries as she talked and was only able to get half of her hamburger down. Brien had no trouble eating and was done in no more than ten minutes. She watched the Adams apple on his throat bob as he drank a soft drink.

"What?" he asked. "I had to drink it fast because I have a paper straw."

"Nothing. I was just watching you, is all."

"Yes, I noticed. You should have been eating instead of using a fry to stir your hamburger."

"I didn't do that."

He started the truck. "Maybe not, but you could have the way you were waving the fries around."

She chuckled. "It's good we're going home. I need to get Roger out; get him moving."

"I like Roger. He's a good boy."

She smiled. "He is. He's such good company, too. Life is far more interesting with a dog."

The sun had just gone down and Faith watched the car lights go by in the opposite lane. "It was a fun night."

"You sound like it's over."

She smiled. "I so enjoyed myself. Thanks so much."

"I had a good time, too. Thank you."

"You didn't mind being in the spotlight? Or, is it under the microscope?" she asked.

"Except for the waitress, I came in not knowing anyone. That happens to people in life. I don't think I suffered too much. I noticed you seemed to keep your attention averted from the crowd."

"Yeah, that's just it, McGrew. I can't remember when I had such a fun time. Maybe when I was a teen."

"That's just sad, you know."

"Yes, I suppose so. But I'm not hiding myself any longer."

"I'm glad to hear that, Faith." He looked down at her feet. "Are your feet cold?"

"No. I can't believe I lost my shoes."

"Oh, they'll turn up. The town's too small for someone to steal them and then wear them around, you know?"

"That's probably true. Just pull up in front of the house, please."

"Of course. Got to walk you to the door."

After unlocking the door, she walked in and Brien entered behind her. "Roger?"

"I thought you let him stay loose in the house."

"I did. Roger?" When he didn't come, or whine or bark, fear gripped her gut. She turned to Brien.

"Do you think you left the back door open, didn't shut it all the way?"

She rubbed her face as if to clear her mind. "I don't think so. But maybe. I could have been thinking too hard about the date."

"Let's look."

Faith walked behind Brien to the door. It stood ajar.

"How stupid of me," she said.

He gave the door a push and said, "Let's look around the house and make sure we're alone here. Then I'll go look for Roger. Don't worry."

"Okay." Faith continued to follow him through the house, then back to the main floor.

"You're sure nothing's disturbed, right?" he asked at length.

She shook her head. "I don't think so. But frankly, right now I'm worried about Roger. He should be here on the porch. It's a distance to a neighbor's house. This is awful."

"I'll look around outside, then drive down the road. We'll find him." He hurried outside. She could hear him calling, quieter now as he moved down the road.

The back door banged shut and she froze. She turned her head toward the door, straining to hear any other sounds. She thought Brien had already shut the door. After searching her brain frantically, she remembered that he gave it a push, the kind of action that most assuredly should have shut the door.

Not hearing anything else, she let out a breath and rubbed her hands along the sides of her jeans. She continued to listen for Brien to call out or any sound of Roger, but all was quiet.

She heard a hard knock at the back door, and jumped

back, so startled her heart pounded. Instead of standing there worrying, she moved slowly to the back door.

Marty Walker stood at the door holding her sandals with two fingers. "The door was open," he said. "The manager said you were looking for your shoes. I happened to see them along the wall back by the drums. They're a pretty nice pair. Thought you'd want them back."

Something told her all was not well, so she kept her distance. "You can just set them down right there. Thank you very much, Marty. How nice of you to travel all the way out here at this time of night."

"I think you'd do the same for me."

Not at this time of night, she wouldn't. "Thanks again." Making the tone of her words sound final.

"Okay. I'll bid you goodnight," he said at length.

"Goodnight, Marty. Drive safely." But where was his vehicle? she wondered.

aith looked away as not to encourage him and listened for the door to shut and when it did, she let out a labored breath. She'd grab her sandals and set them on the stairs to take upstairs after Roger came home.

She took a step toward the back door, then stopped abruptly. Marty stood back to the right of the door. She attempted to speak but nothing came out. On her second attempt, she said, "Oh, oh, oh good. I…I was going to ask you if you'd seen my dog. Uh, have you seen him?"

"Yes."

He walked to her and for the life of her she couldn't back away. "Oh…where?"

Marty reached down as if to pick up something but grabbed her ankle instead and she fell back like a fallen tree.

He'd knocked the wind out of her. When she could breathe, she said, "Oh! That hurt."

Sitting down next to her, his hand just under her throat, he said, "It was meant to hurt. You've been a bad, *bad* girl tonight. Dancing around and throwing yourself at that man like… Well, you might as well just walk the streets. That's not the impression I want my girl to give to the town."

"No!"

"I can feel your heart pounding. You're feeling very alive, aren't you?" He pressed down harder.

She decided maybe she shouldn't speak.

"Aren't you?" His voice sounded wild, passion filled, with low threatening tones.

She nodded several times, feeling a load of regret of what could have been. In her mind, she prayed to God like there was no tomorrow, because that was quite possible. In what could be her last moments her mind flashed to how she'd gone to church and believed in God, but she suddenly realized she'd believed in herself just as much.

She had prayed hard for her teaching award and to be mayor, but that was all. How foolish to think she had any real power over her own life? Apparently, she'd only thought He was a strong influence. What she should have been doing was praying adamantly for her father who was making major changes in his life, whether to marry Gwen and where to live. Perhaps she'd preferred to hide out in the woods, afraid she could fool herself but not anyone else. She was so sorry now. "I'm sorry," she said far more to God than to Marty.

"Well, you should be," he ground out. "Say it again."

She jerked at his tone. "I am sorry."

"That's better."

*Roger, where was Roger?* Her beloved Roger. "Where's Roger?"

"Roger? Is that your lover's name?"

"No. That's my dog. Where is he?" Tears poured out of her, realizing he'd probably killed him.

"Your stupid dog?"

She nodded, because she couldn't speak.

"I didn't hurt him if that's what you mean. I just let him off back toward town."

"He's not my lover," she said.

"What? Oh. The way you were acting with that man tonight, I'd say you're lying."

She shook her head, adamantly.

"Well, that's good, but you'll have trouble convincing the town of this. And I don't appreciate the place you've put me in."

"What place is that?" she asked wincing when he growled.

"Trying to improve your image."

"Oh," she said quietly.

With a hand, he grabbed part of her hair and jerked.

"Roger, Roger," she said through tears, not believing this man could be kind to her dog. She prayed for Roger, feeling compelled to do so.

He slapped her face. "Pay attention to me. You're going to have to start paying attention to me. Right now, Faith. Now stand up."

The weight of despair made it hard for her to stand, so he jerked at her arm and pulled her toward the back door. Where are we going?" she asked, then flinched.

"I'm taking you to my house. I'm going to make you see that I'm the only one for you." His thumb stabbed toward his chest in emphasis. "Not some pretty boy, fly by night. You need someone from this town to take care of you, so you don't start making a fool of yourself again."

"I promise I won't make a fool of myself again," she said quietly.

"No, you won't, because you are coming with me." The screen door slammed behind them.

"Please, let me stay. I will be good."

He stopped and pulled her face close to his, she could smell his stale breath as he said, "You are just like my wife.

Pleading, pleading. Well, she's dead now, so take that as a warning."

~

Brien started his truck and then punched 911 into his phone. When he hung up, he checked the truck's mileage and noted that he'd traveled about a mile from Faith's house. He pulled to the side of the road and hopped out of his truck. "Roger! Roger!"

He'd heard nothing but crickets, silent now. After opening the truck door, he put a foot up and settled back inside. At three miles from the house he met two police cars. He blinked his front lights and one of the cars stopped for him.

Detective Holly Mason stepped out and up to his open window. He did his best trial work to make Holly see that whatever was happening to Faith had to stop.

Holly's eyebrows furrowed as she listened, then said, "Why are you out here and not with Faith?"

"I searched the house and then came out here looking for Roger." As if to prove what Brien said was true, Roger ran up between them.

"Oh, good boy, Roger. Good boy." Brien rubbed his head and then Roger jumped up on him as if to give him a hug. He opened the door of his truck and Roger hopped in.

"I have a K-9 cop with me in the police car that went up ahead," said Holly. "He'll search out the woods around the house and see if anyone is camping a little too close to Faith."

Brien nodded. "I have a trailer in the claim next to her house, but that is all I've seen."

"Okay. You two follow me," she said and opened the door of the police cruiser and sat inside.

Roger nuzzled Brien's ear as Brien spun the truck around and went off after the police. After Holly's words, he felt a deep dread settling over him, thinking that he'd been wrong to come looking for Roger. He should have stayed with Faith. Brien believed he'd not be able to forgive himself if something had happened to that sweet girl. How could he be so stupid?

Back at the house, Brien kept Roger in the truck, not wanting him to interfere with anything the police dog needed to do.

He also wanted to go search himself and decided he'd start off immediately behind the back of the house.

"Stay here, Brien," said Holly. "Let's get some flood lights going," she added to an officer near her.

"I can't," Brien said. "I've got to go find her."

"No, your emotions are involved."

"And that is why I need to go."

"Come here," she said. "Listen to me."

He turned toward Holly, leaned in her direction, but didn't move closer.

"You need to fill your role as her attorney. If you are involved any more than you are, there's a good chance you won't be allowed to serve her in this way."

He straightened, not entirely convinced.

"I know that you are an extraordinary man when it comes to your chosen profession. Use your gift for Faith. Use your gift for *her*."

FAITH HAD NEVER BEEN SO scared and didn't realize it was possible to be frightened enough to tremble. She strained to listen to the sounds of the night, hoping to hear Brien. Yet, her mind told her no, she didn't want anything to happen to him. Marty had adrenaline pumping through his tense body and could be deadly dangerous.

They walked away from the house and road and into the woods, Marty jerking her arm if she stumbled. She found it hard to remedy that due to the darkness, the rocky path and frequent bushes. He growled again when she stumbled to her knees and almost toppled him over.

"Come on, you can do better than that. You're stalling, aren't you?"

"No! No. I'm really not. It's hard to see and you're pulling my arm so I can't balance well."

"Don't. Talk. Back." He pulled again and she stumbled and dropped down on one knee but her anger at being treated subhuman strengthened her.

She righted herself before he could hit her with the arm he'd pulled back in a striking position. She grabbed a branch and while maneuvering ahead let it flap back and hit Marty's face. Pretending to stumble, she stooped and fumbled for a rock. Her nails dug into the soil as she worked a rock the size of her palm into her hand. She pressed the rock to her chest and she stood. Gaining a like confidence, she took her free hand and shook her arm before pointing her elbow and driving it into Marty's stomach.

He bent and moaned while she lifted the rock over her heart.

"You don't want to do that. You'll be mighty sorry, if you do."

"I'll be mighty sorry if I don't," she said back, and the rock grazed his head. Enough to get him on all fours.

With a burst of energy, she decided to run, but fell all too soon when Marty grabbed her leg and she fell hard on her shoulder.

Marty slugged her in the eye before covering her body with his body. Unrelenting pain throbbed in her shoulder.

He grew eerily quiet and she struggled to free any part of her.

*Where was Roger?* Her heart grew heavy at the thought of his death but felt an inkling of optimism when she thought she heard panting. He'd apparently heard it too, because he lifted his head and listened before struggling to pull her straight in front of him into a sitting position, his hands now tight at her elbows.

Hope filled her chest as the panting grew with the sound of bush branches pressed down, snapping. Yet, Marty drew a hunting knife from somewhere and held it up toward her face. She knew he meant for her to be quiet, so she stifled a scream.

Roger was upon them and she heard what sounded like human footsteps in the near distance. She leaned forward and away from Marty's torso as the dog's teeth grabbed at his pant leg and Marty's knife waved in the air.

No, it wasn't Roger, he would have come to greet her. It was a German shepherd. Now, Faith thought of nothing but pushing him down as he struggled to stand and get away. When he was off balance, she pushed, and Marty went down hard. The knife flew out of his hand. The dog stood on his chest, barking down at him like a trained police dog, holding his subject at bay.

The light of the moon shined upon the knife on the ground and she grabbed it and stood back.

"Give me the knife," Marty said to her with exasperation, as if he expected her to snap to and obey.

Faith didn't reply, only gripped the knife with her right hand in case she had to use it.

She could hear someone panting behind her as he approached.

The policeman zip tied Marty's hands as he bellowed something about a devil dog that Faith should have knifed.

"Get him off me!" he yelled.

The dog backed off when the policeman grabbed Marty's feet and zip tied them as well. The officer radioed a woman, whose voice sounded like Holly and they waited for the team to gather.

## CHAPTER 19

*B*rien waited inside on Faith's couch, Roger laying on his feet. Roger wasn't sleeping he noted, but rather looking out with worried darting eyes, obviously wondering where his master was. He felt the same way. His heart was full of Faith, to say the least, a feeling new to him.

They'd been there for more than thirty minutes, a long time for Roger and Brien. He'd prayed and hoped and prayed some more that Faith was all right.

When Holly returned to the house with Faith, Brien stood. His eyes filled with tears because Faith's countenance didn't look as frail and white as he'd pictured in his mind's eye. Yet she did have a bruise covering one side of her face and a discolored eye, the white corner now a dark red. Then she started crying and toppled over on Roger, now half weeping and half laughing as she wrapped her arms around a rotating and bouncing animal. He felt jealousy; jealous of a dog and he smiled at the thought and how loving this inter-action was.

Holly stood back at the door as if waiting for Faith to greet them both. He appreciated that.

Faith flew to Brien, dog at her heels and hugged him ferociously. He kissed the top of her head while she cried into his chest. At length he said in little more than a whisper, "Faith, Holly is still here, let's see what else she needs."

"Faith, we need some pictures. Let's go into the bathroom where the light is good and take some pictures of your injuries."

"I will be here as long as you need me, Faith. Go on."

She nodded and went with Holly. They were close enough that he could hear her grunt when she moved a certain way. He rubbed his chin, hating this and again felt guilty for not being with her when Marty grabbed her.

Faith's phone rang. Apparently, she had left it in the house. It was on the dining room table.

"Don't answer her phone," Holly called out to Brien. "She doesn't need anyone in this goldarn town talking to her for a while."

"Okay." He wondered if he should take her away somewhere. He'd have to be patient, he realized. *Perhaps he needed to call her father?*

"I'm taking Faith to the ER, then to the police station."

Brien stood. "Oh?"

"Would you like Brien to come with you?"

"No. I'd like him to stay here with Roger until I get back."

"Are you sure?" he asked.

"Yes. Do you mind waiting with Roger?"

"No, I'll be here. Take your phone and call me, if you need me."

"I will."

Holly said, "You don't answer the phone for anyone else, Faith."

"Do you want me to call your dad?" he asked.

"No...I'll talk to him tomorrow. That will be a better time for me."

He didn't like watching Faith leave the house without him, but then she was merely his friend at this point. He hadn't talked to her about being anything else. He'd have to trust that she knew what she needed for the moment.

He laid back on the couch and looked up at the ceiling and thought about what he wanted in a job. He'd been shaping his future ever since he'd talked to Faith and before he'd found the gold. She'd helped him understand some of Pop's beliefs and how he wanted to be like him, having a relationship with God, not just the nature He'd created. Thankfully, the money Pop had planted for him helped in every way. Now, he just had to sew up some loose ends and then move forward with his plans. Still, some of it depended on what Faith wanted to do.

Brien went to Faith's desk and took a small tablet out of a drawer, along with a pencil. When he sat back down on the couch, Roger joined him, intent on what he had in his hands. "Sorry, it's not food, boy. Wait, you probably want some food, don't you? Come on, we'll find some."

FAITH WALKED into the house and sat next to Brien, nearly on him as if she needed to know if he moved in any way. Holly stood over them, watching, looking from one face to another.

"Are you going to be all right?" Holly asked.

Faith nodded. "I am now." She patted Roger's head and then kissed it.

"Brien, can you stay here with her tonight?" Holly asked.

"Yes, I don't think I can sleep anyway. Can I talk to you a moment?"

"No," Faith said firmly. "You can and will talk in front of me. No secrets. I can take it."

Could she? he wondered. Still, he said, "I want to know if Walker will get out on bail."

"Absolutely not."

"I didn't have a restraining order," said Faith to Brien, regret in her tone.

Holly put a hand on her hip before saying. "Hard to get a restraining order if you don't know who your secret admirer is. He was smart about that, but Faith is going to take care of that tomorrow."

"We'll see who's smarter, him or me," he quipped.

"You're not going to do anything to him, are you Brien? Don't go near him, please," Faith pleaded.

"I am going near him. In court."

"I'm happy you're going to represent Faith."

"No." Faith shook her head repeatedly. "You don't have to do this; you have your own life to live. I'd like you to refer me to someone, though."

"You two can talk about it," said Holly. "I'm going. Faith, you lay back on the couch or go to bed. Get some rest." Holly turned to leave.

"Goodnight," they said in succession and the front door closed.

"I think Marty may have killed his wife," she said to Brien. "Something he said made me think he did it."

"What did he say she died of?"

"He didn't say, but news around town says cancer, but I'm thinking he may have hurried it along."

"They might be able to look into her death then. Rest. We'll talk later. Take a break from work. Nobody will slight you for it."

"You can go, Brien. Don't think that you have to stay."

"How about, I'd be happy to stay? I'm not leaving."

She moved to the side to see his face. "Good. I was hoping you'd stay."

"No place I'd rather be, but under different circum-stances, of course."

"Same here. I do feel talked out though."

"Yes. Understood."

"Can I just lean against you, and listen to you talk?"

"Sure. What would you like to hear about?"

"Uh…how about, what's entailed in passing the bar?"

He chuckled. "You want to go to sleep pretty badly, don't you?"

"I do. I so want this day to end and celebrate a new day tomorrow."

"That's my girl, trying to get back to normal. Okay, glad to help. Well, let's see. I'll start by saying what I heard recently and that is that Oregon is the fourth hardest state to pass. Not that I'm bragging or anything, you know."

"Oh, of course not."

"You don't know how happy I am to be done with that test."

"I think I can imagine."

"Anyway, what I had to know is civil procedure, uh… conflict, agency and partnership. Trust and estates."

"Oh, shoot me…now," she said slowly with hardly any volume.

He tried not to laugh, so he wouldn't disturb her which resulted in holding his breath. After what couldn't be a moment of time, he heard the precious sound of sleep, a longer outlet of breath with barely a trace of whispery sound. He didn't care if he had a kink in his neck in the morning, he cared about being right up next to Faith in the way of a link to her.

When Brien opened his eyes, it was still dark. A wet kiss had jerked him to attention and his heart pounded in antici-pation of more. Sadly, it was Roger who'd licked his cheek and lips.

"Yuck. Roger, no," said Faith.

He guessed Roger wasn't just into him. "Good morning, young lady."

"Thanks. I guess. Sorry about Roger." Faith stood up slowly. "I feel like I've been run over."

"I'm not surprised. You've been through a lot."

"How you doing? Can't be too comfortable on this couch with me and Roger."

"Actually, I'm doing pretty well." Am I? he wondered. "Can I get you something for the pain?"

"No. I'll get it. I need to shower and get ready to go to town. Get a restraining order and a few things from my office. And I need a new phone. I'm going to get a new number. I'll let you know as soon as the number is changed."

"I can come. No problem."

"Not this time. You've done enough. I need to be by myself this morning, try to get my head back in the game, so to speak."

"But you will be coming home by noon, right?"

"Yes, I realize that I need to do that."

"Good. I'll continue to clean up the claim, and then uh... count my money."

She laughed.

"It's nice to hear you laugh again."

"Feels good." She smiled sweetly and angled her head at him. She cleared her throat. "Okay, I will call my dad today too. I know you've been concerned about that. I just don't want him to drop everything and come back here to follow me around wringing his hands. He's finally happy and I don't what to mess that up."

If it wasn't for the bruising on her face, her smile would have been very endearing.

"Faith, you're a good woman. And strong. You'll be okay."

"Thanks, and thanks. I needed to hear that this morning."

"You want me to cook up a mean bowl of cold cereal or something?" he asked.

"No, I'll manage."

FAITH MADE a dash into the mayor's office, grabbed some files, her schedule book and slipped them into a large leather bag. She turned to see Rose enter.

"Hello, Faith. Oh, your face," she said, then nothing for a moment, only looked her over. "I didn't expect to see you here today, hoped you had some work stacked up for me."

"As usual, I do. Right here." She tapped the stack with a finger. "Hello to you, too. And don't worry about my face, it'll heal."

"Like I said, I didn't expect you to be here. Tell me how you're doing. Wait, first I must apologize for suggesting that Marty Walker would be a good man to date. I believe I encouraged him to ask you out. I feel so responsible for what happened to you."

Everyone knows what happens in a small town, Faith reminded herself. "I'm doing okay. Please don't feel responsible at all. Please, Rose. You only had my good in mind. You always have. None of us suspected Marty of anything untoward in the past, you know."

"I guess."

"I will talk with you another time. I'd like to get home, but I have some business I need to attend to this morning, so I must leave. Thanks for coming by, Rose. You don't have to stay and work if you don't want to, since I won't be here to visit with you."

"It's the least I can do for you, dear. I'll stay awhile."

Faith had a lump in her throat when she left Rose. It touched her that Rose cared so much and that she blamed herself for Marty's actions. More than ever, she realized that no one was to blame and didn't think that way at all. Murrayville was filled with her friends and everyone would survive.

# CHAPTER 20

*B*rien worked steadily putting the earth back to normal and then prepared the dry-washer to return to the rental store. His mind, however, labored far more on what had happened to Faith.

Because she had become important to him, he felt victimized too, he supposed. The last thing she needed was for him to dwell on the unfairness or the details of what had happened.

Brien looked up at a billowing cloud and realized he didn't feel like an attorney, had to remind himself repeatedly that he was. He guessed it was because he'd forgotten the end zone in the long scramble to get there. He chuckled, then calmed and tears filled his eyes. "Thank you, God, for getting me this far. Thank you. And while I'm at it, help me lift Faith up right now. And when the time comes, help me defend her the best that I can."

He nodded and sniffed, then took the dry-washer to the back of his truck. He'd return it this morning so he'd be home later for his girl. He only hoped she'd see it that way.

～

BRIEN HAD SHOWERED and then started prepping tacos for lunch. He'd invite Faith to his trailer, a change of pace.

His heart picked up a beat when he heard her car pass by. Not unlike Roger, he hurried over to bid her hello as she stepped out of her car.

"Come over for lunch," he said, a little out of breath.

"Oh, okay. That will be nice," she said, smiling.

"Everything go okay, in town?"

"Better than expected, really. I'll tell you about it over lunch," she said, dismissing him, but he'd take no offense. Roger had turned out to be important to him, too.

When Faith came over, she had changed to white tennis shoes, yoga capris and a pink t-shirt.

"Yum. Tacos. I worked up an appetite this morning. Thanks for this, Brien."

"Good. Welcome."

"Looks like you've been busy outside this morning. I don't see the dry-washer anywhere."

"I returned it this morning."

"I don't know if I should be sad or happy about that," she said with a half-smile.

"You're wondering if I'm about to leave, aren't you?"

"I'd be lying if I said no."

"Well, we do need to talk about that."

She laid her taco down for a moment. She knew this moment was coming and should be used to the idea, but her heart seemed to falter, like she was about to hear some terrible, disturbing news.

Brien, apparently unmoved, took another bite of taco and the rusty-colored, beefy grease dripped down his hand and unto his wrist. He, too, set his taco on his plate and picked up a napkin, rubbed it along his hand and wrist and took a long drag of milk. When he finally got around to looking at her, he asked, "Are you okay?"

"Are you pretending that you don't know what I may be concerned about? Or, do you not understand how I may feel about this?"

His chin went down and his forehead creased. When he looked down, she figured he thought back to the last thing he'd said.

She took a big gulp of air and let it out slowly, while his eyes widened. "I'm sorry I'm being a baby. I always knew I couldn't have you here forever. I will most definitely miss you."

"No, you won't," he said with a smile.

"*What*? Of course, I will. No need to say any more."

"It's just-"

"Nope. No more."

He held a finger in the air. "Faith, stop."

"Okay," she said quietly, feeling so sad that he wouldn't let her say what she needed to say, that she'd miss him until the day she died. Just so he'd know how much she cared.

"I'm not going, Faith. Well, I am but only long enough to get my things and move back here."

She smiled, her eyes filling with tears.

"Let's go for a walk, since you're apparently done eating. This is a reminder that you're going to have to start eating in my presence, by the way. Let's not walk in the woods behind you, but some place different. We'll walk down the road. Roger can enjoy some exercise."

"Okay, okay. Let's get moving, so you can start talking."

Roger looked longingly at the partially full plates on the table but turned to follow them anyway. Soon Roger was out in front of them, taking off as if the Malamute in him was pulling a dog sled.

"Did the treasure, I mean the gold you found change your career goals or something?"

"No, you did. You're my treasure." He patted his chest. "You're deep inside."

"Oh, I'm going to cry. I'm going to cry."

He stopped her, put a hand to the back of her head and pulled her close enough to kiss her cheek.

"I had already decided, when I didn't take the last job offer, that I don't want anyone to choose who I represent. That was before I found the gold." He gazed into her face. "I can take a pro bono case, if I wish, and I'm sure I will want to do that from time to time. Doing that kind of work is how I will give back because I have been given much."

She stopped in her tracks. "I think I understand what you're saying. But where is this practice going to be?"

"Murrayville, of course."

"Are you crazy? What do your parents think, your friends?" she asked, palms up. Roger took a jump at one of her hands and she stopped to pat his head before moving on.

Brien let out a big sigh. "That's the thing. This side of me has been wanting to burst out since I started law school, but I wouldn't let it. The colleagues I have as friends, will never understand. So, I need new friends."

"Most importantly then, your parents. And they think…"

"My dad won't understand, but he'll have to come around. My mother supports whatever is important to me. She will understand and cheer me on, no matter what."

Faith considered his words and hoped, she will understand and cheer me on, no matter what."

She considered his words and hoped that she wouldn't be blamed for his choices.

As if hearing her thoughts, he said, "My job choices don't have anything to do with you, Faith. Don't be thinking that."

"Murrayville?" she asked.

"I like it here. I can do some good here. Murrayville needs you…and me."

She frowned.

"What?" he asked, thumbing his chest. "*I* can't decide where I want to live and for what reasons?" After a long moment, he said, "Politics. I may want to get into politics. At this time, it's only a little glimmer in the back of my mind, so please don't think I'm crazy."

She stopped, put her hands on her knees and laughed. "The jury's out on crazy. Ha. Ha. Get it? Jury, lawyer."

He moaned. "Yes, I get it." Roger jumped at his side, apparently happy they were happy.

They reached the end of the road and turned back toward Faith's home, both of them lost in their own thoughts. He knew she had a lot to process, so he let her think.

"Look we're almost back at the house, had our exercise and Roger's, too."

"Yes, very good."

"Let's go out tonight to celebrate my new work plans."

"Sure." She paused, worried she was at fault for his change of plans, yet unsure of what this new bond between them meant. "All right," she added.

"Six-thirty?"

"Yes."

But she wasn't ready to stop sharing yet. She didn't want to be responsible for pushing them into something, even if he did want to settle in Murrayville. So, what would that look like? What did he expect from her in a relationship? Besides the fact that she was the mayor of Murrayville, she didn't want to live with anyone, ever. Didn't want to share her money or her home with someone who only wanted to "be together." He may not like to hear her views and for all she knew, he would eventually pack up his trailer and get out of town. Yet, better to know this up front, she believed.

Faith would respect his views just as she hoped he'd respect hers.

So, dinner may not only be about celebrating new job plans, but a heart-to-heart about their future, if indeed there was one.

She entered the house happy, but with a heavy heart, because somehow, she knew that this much change could be difficult.

Instead of worrying, she called her father. She made every effort to tell him what had happened to her in a non-emotional, matter-of-fact way, but she sensed that he saw through her plan, as they were both taking the next flight out to get to Murrayville.

She supposed the little girl in her appreciated the idea of her daddy coming to her rescue, but did she really want that? And how would Brien respond?

FAITH LOOKED through her closet for the third time, wanting to find the right thing for her date. How silly that she wanted to please Brien, she thought, since according to him, she already had. She used to dress for success at work, or for the townspeople, she realized. Finally, she had come to the point where she needed, and was finally upon the precipice, of doing what was best for her.

God blessed Faith Chadwick's broken road, she came to understand. And it wasn't just about standing on her own; succeeding on her own. No, she was a fallible human being and needed God. She'd never forget that now. And He'd be with her, whether her father lived close by or whether Brien was the man for her. God was the one for her, first and fore-most. And God help her in what she needed to say tonight.

She closed her eyes and grabbed a top and laid it on the

bed. Green was a good color, she told herself firmly. *See, Faith? God is helping you make the right choices already.*

BRIEN LOOKED down before knocking on Faith's door. He'd bought new jeans and a shirt in town today. The pants were called Italy something, but he liked the slim fit. The shirt was button down with a hint of dress up about it and still light-weight for the summertime.

Faith opened the door and gave him a wolf whistle.

"Just the look I was going for," he said, then walked past her. "You don't look so bad yourself. I like the little curly thingy's in your hair."

"They're called tendrils."

"Good, now I'm in the know."

"And I like the spiky hairs at the top of your head," she said.

"Thank you, Ma'am. Ready to go?"

"Yes, but I'm warning you that I have some things to talk about."

"I do too." He frowned. "Do we need to go for a walk first?"

"No. I'm hungry."

"Okay, let's go."

BRIEN OPENED the tall door at Murrayville Roadhouse for Faith and guided her to a back table. He pulled out a chair and she sat down, while he took the opposite side with his back to the wall. After what happened to Faith, he believed she didn't need to see expressions of pity, or anything else, from the town's people. She had enough to deal with, without that, so he brought her here so she could dance and laugh again. Or, maybe he was only being selfish because he wanted to see her have a good time.

They ordered their food and Faith leaned forward. "I feel I need to explain some things to you, about myself and the way I think."

He put the white cloth napkin across his lap and took a sip of water as he studied her face. "Should I be worried?"

"No, these are my thoughts and nothing that you are responsible for. You are responsible for how you respond, your beliefs, of course."

"Okay, then. What's up?" He noted the waitress hurried back with a bread plate and some cubes of butter, then stood there for a moment. He could only think that she wanted to hear tidbits of the conversation.

"Thanks for being on the ball," he said to her.

"Welcome, sir." After a moment, she dipped her knees and left.

Faith had put a roll on her plate and opened a square tab of butter but pointed her butter knife at Brien. "I want to know what your intentions are, Mr. McGrew."

She'd said it with an Irish accent, and he laughed. "Isn't that your father's job?"

"Best get it over before he gets here, I say."

"You called him then. I knew he'd be coming, as soon as he heard."

"Yes." She frowned then and looked down at her roll, absently he'd say.

"Are you going to eat that roll?"

She looked up, then pointed the knife down but not on the butter. "Don't distract me from finding out your intentions."

"I'll make it easy." He moved his head closer to her face and said quietly, "I love you."

Her face lit up with an ear-to-ear smile, and she set her knife down. "I wasn't expecting that."

"That makes it even better then. I'm glad you put the knife down, by-the-way."

"I can pick it back up."

He noted that she didn't return his words. She'd been through a lot; she may need time. He could give her that. Yet, he could feel the love radiating out of her, could feel it for a while now.

Brien picked up her knife and took a moment to butter her bread. "If nothing else, I'm a gentleman."

"I won't live with you," she said, rather bluntly he thought.

After looking around them, to see if any jaws were slack, he said, "I think you're trying to load me up with things I can change, Faith. You are worrying for nothing. And you worry too much about what others think."

"I won't change my mind. I feel strongly about this. And I know I have been worrying too much about others, but not anymore. Not anymore."

"That's not my intention. To make you worry."

"Be careful the plate is hot," said the waitress as she set his food before him. She set Faith's before her, but Brien didn't think she saw it, her eyes were on him.

"I'm afraid you are going to lose weight," he said, smiled and picked up a fork.

"I think I have already," she said and gave an unexpected sweet smile.

It reminded him of how sweet she was. His heart started pounding and he glanced around the room. The band played a fast song and he had no idea just when it had started.

"Faith."

She took a bite.

"Stand up."

"Why? I'm eating, you told me to eat."

He shook his head in a rather incredulous way, she thought. Apparently, he wanted to dance but she was hungry and finally took a bite. The bite of cheesy burrito was so good. Now he looked adamant. Okay, she'd stand up.

As soon as she did, he put a hand in his pocket, then went down on one knee. This was not funny, and she shook her head and with a hand motioned for him to stand up.

Brien shook his head, again unyielding, so she waited, remembering to not worry about what others thought. As a matter of fact, she only looked at *his* face which had turned almost angelic, then he gave her a grin before saying, "Faith Chadwick, will you marry me?"

She must have mistaken his words over the din of the music. Or, he played some sort of stupid joke at a very bad time. But his face belied her thoughts and the ring box told a story as well.

Still, her heart started to swoon of its own accord, and his face looked adorable again. He meant what he said.

She had so many questions, but she'd not ask them at this moment that seemed so perfect to her, even though it had nothing to do with what she'd imagined would happen in her fondest dreams. In front of God and everyone. It. Was. Perfect.

Nodding wildly, she reached for the box and opened it. In the dim light it was hard to get a good look at the ring, but she could see the diamond in the middle twinkle.

It was if the world stood still as she looked at Brien's smiling face, for a moment at least, then a loud booming of the drums and cheering voices filled the air. Faith jumped, startled, and then looked at smiling faces, all around her. She noticed the cheers and well wishes from the town's people. The roll of the drums sounded again, and she held her left hand up.

Brien surveyed the room, noting the applause and the

genuine caring seen in the faces of both the male and female roadhouse patrons. If he did not know it before, he knew that Faith was famous in this small town. And if not mistaken, some of the glances held a moment of pity in them as well as new joy for her. Certainly, they all knew what had happened to her and by whom. Some of the people also lifted their clapping hands to him, and he felt loved as well.

He enjoyed the ambiance of the town, the idea of a less populated place to live. Now, how could he not want to live here, to love and be loved by them, to help them in their time of need?

There was a third job offer that Brien hadn't told Faith about. Now was the perfect time to tell her about it. After waiting for the volume in the room to go down a few decimals, he said, "I have something else to tell you."

She leaned forward. "You do? Should I be worried?" She'd said it with a smile but frowned when he looked down at his hands.

"I'm a lawyer who cares about how the legal system operates. Fairness is important to me. Laws protect people, even the guilty."

"Of course. You are a man of integrity. What's going on? Just be direct." She took a bite of her burrito.

"This is about your trial," he said and patted her free hand.

"Oh, okay." She looked up from her food to give him eye contact.

"You, Faith, as a victim of a violent crime, will not need a private lawyer. In technical terms, Marty Walker, as a criminal arrested for a violent crime will be prosecuted by the district attorney's office. The district attorney will be protecting your rights, Faith.

"I know that it will be hard for Walker to get a fair trial in this town. But a fair trial is what he'll get, because I will be involved and because a fair trial means a guilty verdict."

Faith shrugged a shoulder. "Wait, I don't get how you will be involved then."

He smiled rather smugly, she thought.

"I've had another job offer."

"What a night. My heart's starting to pound again. What does that mean?"

"I looked into working with the Murrayville County district attorney and landed a job offer. The current DA was way past retirement age but felt he was needed. But, with me coming in, he's retiring."

"Are you sure this is what you want?" she asked and put her fork down.

"It is. It really is."

"Well, good. Congratulations."

He leaned forward and gave her a quick kiss, and then picked up his fork. "Thank you. It's time to protect the people of Murrayville and it's time for me to protect the woman I love by putting Walker behind bars where he belongs."

# ABOUT THE AUTHOR

Mary Vine is an author, publisher, speaker and retired educator. She writes contemporary and historical romantic fiction, a time travel series, and inspirational children's books, the BIG GUY UPSTAIRS, BIJU SILVER LINING and DRAGON GILBY. Mary, and her husband can usually be found in Southwest Idaho or Northeast Oregon.

To learn more about Mary Vine, visit
http://www.maryvine.com/
http://authormaryvine.blogspot.com

OTHER BOOKS BY MARY VINE

**Contemporary Romance**

Maya's Gold

A Place to Land

A Haunting in Trillium Falls

Snake River Rendezvous

**Historical Romance**

Wanting Moore

**Time Travel Series**

Nugget of Time

Goldbrick

Summer Solstice

**Children's Books**

The Big Guy Upstairs

Biju Silver Lining

Dragon Gilby

WINDTREE PRESS

Thank you for purchasing this Windtree Press publication. For other books of the heart, please visit our website at https://windtreepress.com.

Windtree Press
Portland, Oregon